City Suite

Akmed Khalifa

DEDICATION

To all those who call the city home

Illustrations and Photos

Table of Contents

Life in the City

It can be a sweet thing or it can be a funky thing can kiss you on the lips or bite you on the ass or both at the same time be your present or your past show you a glimpse of the future be bitter or sweet or bittersweet be that moment that spot that point in space and time where it all comes together that low down dirty nasty thing you can't forget when something gets put on your mind that changes you forever that grows you up all at once makes you stop bullshitting yourself and everyone else it can happen in the city where life can do it to you all at once from behind or on top of you make you love it or hate it make you feel it in your bones give you the reins smack your pony on the ass and yell gitty-up.

You Were There

The city

streaked red yellow blue

its skin wet in summer rain

breathed

took folks up at the corner

exhaled us one by one at the end of the block

alone

umbrella in hand

beneath scattered streetlight

in the middle of 55th

between the puddles and the pavement

in the marrow of that dark night

I thought of you and only you

Nothing to Smile About

Life goes on in the city, and no one knows anybody or anything outside of his or her own tight circle of humanity, and at times no one cares.

Consider this. Across the street from one of many vacant lots lives, a kid named Paul. He rarely smiles. He has nothing to smile about. He is twelve, or thirteen, or fourteen, hell, he doesn't know. No one knows for sure how old he is. They always guess. He is tall, slightly muscular, and most often wears a scowl on his face. His mother had abandoned him shortly after he was born. She was a crackhead, and he was born addicted to cocaine. No one knows who his father is.

As Paul grew up in the bowels of orphanages and temporary shelters for unwanted waifs, he was often cold and hungry. He was the crack baby that no one wanted to adopt. He became increasingly resentful each time he was ignored by potential parents, and time slowly etched a scowl on his face. That scowl became the only part of himself that he treasured. It was his; no one could take it away. Shortly after his fifth birthday, he was assessed as having a behavioral disorder, and in each school he attended, he was put into special education classrooms. Students at these schools shunned him and the students in his classrooms and often called them emo kids: those who were emotionally out of control.

Paul has one friend, Rosco, a thug who hangs out in poolrooms perfecting his pool hustle and who runs the street with a gang of other tough kids. Rosco befriended Paul because he thought he looked like his younger brother, who lives in some forgotten place in the world, with people who want him to forget everything about his thuggish older brother. Paul only sees Rosco when he sneaks out of the house he is staying in with his foster parents. He gets moved around a lot. He's been moved from foster home to foster home by child welfare agencies as he has grown up. The foster care system is tough on young boys, especially young black boys who had been crack babies, and who scowl most of the time.

Paul wants to remain angry at the world. He doesn't want to forget the pain and struggle life has brought him. He would bare his emotional scars if he could. That's what his face shows the world, things he can't say. Paul doesn't want to be happy. He is afraid to be happy because he knows it won't last. As soon as he starts smiling, someone takes away his reason for smiling, so his angry face greets the world. He smiled once while playing with a toy in one of the nondescript places he was forced to call home, and a bigger kid took it away from him. Paul beat that boy over the head with a can of spray starch he found sitting on an ironing board in the room they were in. Paul was moved out of that home, and never again saw the boy he had beaten or the toy he had been happily playing with.

Paul wants out of the foster care system. He wants to make money gambling in poolrooms like his friend Rosco. He is eager to go it alone on the streets. He is biding his time until he turns eighteen. Then he will jump into the streets and earn fast money, and hang out with fast women he had heard about and seen from time to time. Then he will smile. Then he will have things to smile about that no one can take from him. Then he will dare them to try.

Erstwhile Turnipseed

Now, it should go without sayin', but I'm gonna say it any way. Any child born with a name like Erstwhile Turnipseed is gonna have to fight his way through a heap of his boyhood years. That's what I was named, and the fact that I'm a dark-skinned Negro probably didn't help either.

I guess you could say that I'm about as dark-skinned as a person could be without havin' to find a made-up color to describe the flesh that's coverin' his bones. I used to ask my momma and daddy why they picked a name like Erstwhile for a dark skinned boy like me anyhow, but I ain't never got a satisfactory answer outa them. My momma always said it was my God-given name, and my daddy always told me that it would prove itself to me one day and that I'd be glad and proud to be called Erstwhile Turnipseed.

They might as well have called me Meanwhile. That woulda made more sense. I woulda realized that I had to wait to see what I might turn out to be with a name like that. Yeah, Meanwhile Turnipseed, that's a name that a kid can wait to grow into, or at least understand that he had to wait, but Erstwhile Turnipseed didn't make no sense to me. They spared my two brothers and my sister. They named my brothers Thomas, and Joshua, and my sister May. They say misery loves company, and I woulda enjoyed my sister's company if they had named her Maybe. Just two little letters at the end of May and we could have defended our names together, but no, they got more sensible with her and my brothers, leavin' me to pound my way outa childhood one fist at a time, all by my lonesome.

I was glad when we moved up South from Georgia to Pennsylvania. It was a few years before the civil rights movement started all over the country, and Negros had it hard in the South. I thought it would be easier on a boy like me in the North, but it wasn't much difference. I mean, there weren't no colored and white signs over bathroom doors and water fountains, but there were places colored folk weren't allowed in, and everyone knew it. The signs were in everyone's head, which made it seem worse to me. It was just a little better on a dark-skinned kid in the Negro community I lived in. Colored folk didn't actually bring out the brown paper bag for you to hold the back of your hand next to, so they could see if you were light enough to be allowed into their parties and social gatherins'. The brown paper bag was still in a lot of folk's minds. They just made up some excuse like your name wasn't on the list.

We moved into a tough part of the city of Pittsburgh, Pennsylvania where all the kids had more sensible names like George, and Willie, and James, which still left me on the school battleground instead of the playground at recess, but I got used to fightin' my way through all the name callin', and got to be pretty tough. Soon I was big enough and bad enough to keep everybody cept them that was bigger and tougher than me from makin' fun of me, and after a while, even they got tired of takin' me on.

I'll never forget the best fight and the best win of my school days, and it wasn't on the playground, or in the streets. It was in the school auditorium. I had managed to get myself into a geography contest between the sixth-grade class of my school and the sixth grade class of a school way on the other side of town, where kids lived in a place called Pleasant Hills. It got that name on accounta all the money the people who lived there had and how much better they thought they were than everyone else. Although I fought a lot and came from a poor family, a family that I got a lot of love and support from, I was no dummy, and I loved maps and places around the world. I knew more about geography than any other kid in my class, and that got me into the contest. I didn't want to join it, but when my teacher said that the kids we would go up against were from a high-class part of town, and the winner got twenty-five bucks, I was all in.

The day of the contest started out normal, I guess, cept that I got up early, and started readin' a geography book my teacher gave me to prepare myself. My momma was already in the kitchen makin' fried apples with nutmeg and cinnamon and bakin' biscuits, and after wolfin' down a man-sized plate of food and a glass of milk, I was off to school to talk to my teacher about the contest. My momma hugged me and wished me luck, and I met my daddy at the front door, comin' home from doin' a extra night shift at the steel mill. He told me that even though he would be tired as all get out, he and the whole family would be there to cheer me on.

When I got to school, I went straight to Miss Taylor's room. She was our contest coach and everybody's favorite teacher, especially the boys, cause she was young and pretty, and tree-top tall. She was also one of only three Negro teachers in the whole school. Miss Taylor was glad to see me and happy to see that I was in good spirits, especially when I told her that I couldn't wait to take on all them high-class kids from the other side of town. She sat me down in a chair and gave me some advice. She warned me that there might be some laughter when they called my name, and the kids might continue to snicker while I was givin' my answer to a question. She told me not to let it bother me. She also told me that the guy askin' the questions was not a nice man, but if I wanted to win I had to be tough-minded. She knew I could handle myself with my fists, but this time I would only have my mind to go into battle with.

It was finally time to go to the auditorium to start the contest. We got together backstage, and everybody was pinned with a number, and last-minute advice buzzed through the air like a swarm of Honey Bees headed for a flower patch. The curtain opened and we all walked to the seats that our numbers were taped to. The announcer, Mr. Poindexter, talked about the rules and told everyone how the contest was supposed to work. Then to my surprise, he called my number first. Miss Taylor said that I would be eighth or ninth in line for a question. I stood up and walked to the center of the stage. Mr. Poindexter looked down at a sheet of paper he was holdin' in his hand and then looked up with a smirk on his face.

"Uh, is this right, Erstwhile? Is this an error? Is your name Erstwhile Turnipseed?

A whole lot of people laughed, and the kids on the stage snickered just like Miss Taylor said they would.

"That's right, Erstwhile Turnipseed," I answered with a evil stare.

"Okay," he said and cleared his throat. "Erstwhile Turnipseed," he said again with a funny accent, and people laughed again. "What is the largest continent in the world?"

I wanted to say, "Your momma's fat behind," but out in the audience, I saw my daddy starin' straight at me with a serious look on his face like he did whenever he expected me to do the right thing, and I answered, "Asia."

"That is correct, Erstwhile Turnipseed," and again, the laughter filled the auditorium.

It went on like that for at least half of the contest until everyone realized that I wasn't just a dumb colored boy with a funny name and that I knew my geography facts. Then they started to clap every time I gave a answer that was right. I stood up every time my name was called and gave the right answer until it got down to just me, and one of them snob kids.

"Harold, what is the longest river in the world?' Mr. Poindexter asked.

"The Nile River," he said.

"That is incorrect, Harold. Erstwhile Turnipseed, if you answer this question correctly, you will win our geography contest. What is the longest river in the world?"

"The Amazon," I said.

"That is correct," he said. The audience stood and clapped, and my family stood, and clapped, and smiled, and my daddy put his hands together and raised them over his head like they do for prizefighters after they win a boxin' match. He was very proud of his son, and I was really happy. I had made my family proud of me. I was the first Turnipseed to ever win a contest like that, and we got twenty-five dollars for it. That was a great day and a great night. My momma cooked my favorite meal, and my family had a great time at home.

But it still wasn't the day when I was proudest to be named Erstwhile Turnipseed. That didn't come until I had hung the sign over the front door of my new business. It was a simple sign and read "Erstwhile Turnipseed, Plumber."

My seven-year-old son walked up to me and said, "Hey, Dad, that's a good sign. I want you to change my name to Erstwhile so I can be just like you, Erstwhile Turnipseed, Plumber."

Will The Real Dope Fiend Please Stand Up?

Hardcore heroin addicts, real dope fiends, have trouble standin' up-a lot. They nod a lot, scratchin', diggin' at their skin, and yeah, they fall a lot, out of chairs, out of a lean against a wall, out of a dream or two, or three. Yeah the dreams, when they're high, when they're loaded, floatin' on that doojie, smack, horse, dreams so real that the real world isn't the desirable location anymore. They want to get back to the land of nod and stay in that high ass wonderland. So, standing up ain't shit. It's the nod, the lean, the dope stupor that they want. And yeah they don't want to be sick like it is when they can't get fixed when the connection ain't comin' round the corner.

How do I know this? Cause I've been there, on the corner watchin' the dope deals go down, watchin' them tie off in the ride, watchin' them nod and dream, and scratch and lean.

I was there when Elbow Pratt (got his nickname from elbowin' his way through fistfights at an early age) overdosed, damn near died, was layin' on the floor with his eyes rolled up in his head, couldn't see nothin' but the white part. We stood him up, walked him around, put him in the tub, and filled it with cold water. He was doin' the dope death crawl, gettin' his body ready for the boneyard. We got some ice cubes and pushed them down his pants, but he was slowly checkin' out, had bought a one-way ticket outa life in the hood. Then Harper got his works unjammed, filled the syringe with saltwater and shot it into his veins. Pratt gasped, his eyes rolled back down out of his head, he was in dope heaven, the place every junkie wants to be, comin out of an overdose, alive and as high as they could ever be on earth and still be alive. He was incoherent, and we left him there, alive and in a deep nod, and he started scratchin', diggin' in his skin and no doubt crawlin' through countless dreams.

But that's just one of many dope fiend stories about Elbow Pratt. One day or I should say one mornin', early as hell, the sun was still coppin' some z's under the horizon some damn where. Pratt was on his way to work, yeah, dope fiend work, lookin' for someone or somethin' to rip off, when he walked past the drug store. The thought occurred to him that he was standin' in front of a junkie's gold mine; after all they called it a drug store.

Instead of hustlin' to get some money to buy some H from the dope man, why not steal the drugs from the drug store? They gotta have some first-class morphine inside.

He crept close to the back door, looked around a couple of times, and then smashed through the back window with his fist, but the window had safety glass in it, with wire in between two panes of glass. The wire ripped through his skin and tore into veins and arteries in an arm where the veins and arteries were messed up from years of shootin' dope: an arm that had skin that looked like the train tracks runnin' from South Philly to New York. His life was saved that time by the burglar alarm and the Rollers. Yeah, that's what we called the police, cause they usually rolled up on us unexpectedly. Anyway, the Rollers saw him fall on the avenue, bleedin', losin' blood like he was tryin' to rinse the pigeon shit off the sidewalk.

They called for an ambulance, and soon, Elbow was on his way to the emergency room. He had five hours of surgery, to save his life and repair the damage to his left arm. The bets on the street were that he wouldn't be shootin' dope in that arm again. After they pulled him out of surgery they pushed him into an area of the hospital sometimes used for patients with security issues, where they could be easily watched, but they weren't prepared to watch hard-core dope fiends.

So, later that same day, that night in fact, I be-bopped into the poolroom, and my jaw dropped to the floor when I saw Elbow with a cast on his arm damn near up to his neck. He was playin' nine ball, shootin' pool with one arm, tryin to hustle enough money to get high, to shoot some heroin into his body somewhere. After he nearly croaked on the sidewalk in front of the drug store, after five hours of surgery, after crawlin' out of the window in the security recovery ward at the hospital in a hospital gown, this cat was workin' to feed his habit. That's how dope fiends are. They're committed to gettin' high, and they're master schemers. Just think, if they put as much effort into doin' the right thing, into makin' honest money, they would be role models for success. But the dope jones drives them. The power of the high, the march to the nod, the lean, the stupor, makes them relentless. I don't know about everything they do to scoop up cash to get high, but I do know that some of their schemes are brilliant. They can make somethin' out of what seems like nothin'.

For instance, I cut into Smurf Collins on the sidewalk one day. Now, Smurf got his name cause he turned blue one day when he was over dosin' on some killer dope. By the way, they called the dope he damn near died from Smurf Snuff and every junkie in the city tried to buy some of it. You would think the opposite would be true, that these cats would be runnin' away from some dope that almost killed somebody. But remember what I said earlier, when a fiend ODs and doesn't die, he is as high as he could ever be, and that's what all the junkies in town were hopin' for after Smurf almost got snuffed by that doojie.

Anyway, I saw him standin' on the bus stop, and he was holdin a bunch of bus transfers in his hand.

"You plannin' on ridin' the bus all day or what?" I asked.

"Hell to the naw," he said. "This is my new hustle."

"So how are you makin' money from bus transfers?"

"Hey man, it costs two dollars and twenty-five cents to ride the bus durin' rush hour, and if you ain't transferin' you just get off at your stop. I yell at the window and ask people who get on with a transfer if I can have it if they're through with it. All the transfers have some time left before they expire. Then I sell the transfer for a dollar to people at the stop who are goin one place and just need to pay when they get on the bus. They save a dollar and twenty-five cent, and I make a dollar. I made thirty-seven dollars already baby. I'll be on my way to the dope man's crib in a minute."

"How long you been doin this, man?

"For a couple weeks. It's a nice hustle, but it ain't gonna last long. I know some other dope fiends are gonna find out what I'm doin' and it'll get crowded at the bus stop. Everyone will be tryin' to creep into my game, and then the Rollers'll shut it down, even though we ain't doin' nothin' to hurt nobody."

"That's a helluva hustle man. How did you come up with this?"

"I was just sittin' across the street from the bus stop one day, and I saw people throwin' away their transfers after they got off the bus. Then I put two and five together and fixed this scheme so I could get a fix, and I been doin' it ever since."

"You oughtta be runnin' your own business, man. You would be rich by now."

"I don't wanna be rich. I just wanna be high."

Dope is some powerful shit. It runs the lives of junkies all over the country. A lot of them get on it and can't get off, ride that white horse to death, usually theirs. And sometimes their dream world spills over into the real world like a nightmare, like the time I walked into Rudy's poolroom on the Avenue one Friday night. It was like a scene out of some new bizarre movie, some slow-motion 3D flick, some weird graphic comic book. Everybody but Rudy was high. They were all noddin' and scratchin', diggin in their skin, leanin' at different angles. Some cats were slowly fallin' out of chairs; some were slidin' down the wall. A couple were leanin' over the pool table with a pool stick in their hands. One was comin' out of the bathroom, stopped in the middle of pullin' his pants up to go into a deep nod. It was the scariest shit I've ever seen, and as I backed out of the poolroom, I yelled at the top of my lungs, "Will the real dope fiend, please stand up?"

The Warming of Cool Walter Meadows

Walter was as cool as they come, smooth and silky, wore his hat like it was designed with him in mind, slightly broken in, cocked ace deuce, accompanied by a fifteen-degree tilt of his head as he strolled effortlessly down city streets and avenues. He was never stressed. No one had ever seen him flustered. He became known as the personification of smooth things, of fluid, tranquil, flowing things.

Walter was a serious-minded individual. He didn't involve himself in frivolous, useless pursuits, in distractions leading nowhere, in purposeless time killing silly things, in fruitless activities, in efforts ending in carefree frolic. Walter didn't play. He threw his radio away because it played.

Walter had been cool, so long folks in the community couldn't remember when he wasn't. To many of them, it seemed as though he had been born chilly. And that was his attitude about any and everything. He just hadn't found anything to become passionate or concerned about. Walter was asked one day why he played the game of life so coolly. His reply was, "I don't play the game I work the game, baby, smooth as hell. I don't sweat. It might leave a water spot on my threads."

In customary fashion, Walter was coolly sauntering across a large parking lot one mid-summer afternoon, not paying much attention to anything, and particularly not the crowd of people gathered at the north end of the lot looking toward the avenue. A couple of them pointed at an approaching object moving at a fast clip down the hill. Walter briefly noted their behavior but wasn't interested in what they could possibly be looking at. Besides, it just wouldn't be hip for him to join the crowd.

However, unbeknownst to Walter, several steep blocks away, two adventurous young boys, after accepting a double dare from friends, were on a raggedy old bike flying down one of the most treacherous hills in Pittsburgh. It was long and steep with a couple of hellacious turns so sharp that you couldn't see approaching traffic beyond the wide bends, traffic notorious for speed and disregard for anyone or anything in its way.

They zoomed down the last block before the intersection and were heading toward fast-moving traffic on the avenue. Walter happened to look up and see them approaching the intersection. There was not much time to think. Walter acted in an instant, did something he had never done, moved faster than anyone with memory of his chilled history could recall. He made a dash toward the intersection, without a plan, didn't have a clue what he would or could do. He was just motivated to act.

The two boys and their bike, hurtling toward an inevitable collision with thousands of pounds of moving metal and glass, were powerless to stop their forward motion. Frightened beyond reason, scared past rational thought, out of touch with reality, one of them decided to exit the rear of the bike. He dropped the tire pump he had been holding onto, cast it aside, pitched it from his left hand, and used his right hand to push off of the bike frame. He was immediately bounced several times off of the pavement and heaved back onto the sidewalk in front of the little community convenience store they had just passed. He had traveled six or seven yards backward as his body flipped through the air. He had been knocked unconscious but, miraculously, was not seriously injured.

The other boy, shocked that his riding partner had leaped from the back frame of the bike, continued to pump the brakes, to no avail. Meanwhile, Walter was streaking toward the intersection in an effort to do something he hadn't a clue of. Bystanders who had the entire scene in their view were surprised to see Walter dashing into action. Nearing the intersection, Walter had realized what he had to do. He had to stop the traffic so that this kid and his bike could make it through the intersection unharmed. Walter jumped into the middle of the intersection and held out his arms with his open palms facing the traffic in both directions. Tires screeched as drivers applied their brakes. Walter had gained just enough time for the bike and its last passenger to zip through the intersection, but one vehicle could not stop in time before hitting Walter, knocking him several feet into the air. He crashed back down onto the pavement in the middle of the street.

People rushed to where Walter lay struggling to breathe the hot summer air through the blood gushing from his nose. One leg was bent behind his back. Having softly crash-landed into a group of shrubs in front of a small manicured lawn, the bike's now safe passenger ran back toward the intersection.

Walter bleeding on the asphalt, in the blistering heat of the August afternoon, never felt more alive. He had always been too hip to interact. He had never been moved enough to associate with those he considered squares. But on this day, in this moment, Walter's actions bonded him forever to the lives of two young boys, and an entire community that would warm and keep the memories of him alive in ways his coolness never could.

It Was Nothing at First

It was nothing at first, just a clink, and a bump, nothing enough to distract Marshall as he reached inside the refrigerator for the final ingredient of another taste sensation.

Marshall, a factory worker at the auto assembly plant about a mile from his home, lived alone in a large two-bedroom apartment that he kept rather neat and clean. He had one bad habit. Food often sat in his refrigerator for months at a time until it dried or exploded in its container. Marshall, young, smart, and headed back to junior college in the fall, considered himself a mixologist, someone who could combine multiple flavors and items to create gourmet like food. This time he just needed the mayo to slather over the three-decker samich he had constructed on the kitchen counter. He drooled in anticipation as he wrapped his mitt around twelve hundred calories of munch and crunch, that would soon be oozing between his fingers, and back down onto the paper plate from which it had risen.

Again came the clink, and bump, louder this time, and accompanied by a thump, and a clank. But no matter, Marshall sunk his teeth into the gathered vittles in his hands and savored the blended sensation he had created.

Devouring his midday treat and wiping his mouth, Marshall leaned back in the kitchen chair, satiated and pleased that he was able to create a feast from nondescript items in his refrigerator.

Ah, that was good as it gets. The only thing I could have done better was to have had someone make it for me.

Clank, clank, thump, clink, clack.

What the hell is that?

Marshall looked around the kitchen.

Damn, I bet I got a mouse in here somewhere.

He rose from the kitchen table and edged toward where the sound had seemed to come from. Clack, clackity, clink, clinkity, thump.

It's comin' from the refrigerator.

He edged close enough to the refrigerator to put his ear to the door.

How did a mouse get into the refrigerator, and how the hell do I get it out?

Marshall knew he needed something other than his hands if he were to get a mouse out of his refrigerator. He would have to find it first and then trap it in some kind of container in order to remove it. His eyes wandered around the kitchen for a brief moment until he spied a large, half-empty jar of peanut butter on the counter. He had found his trap.

I'll open it, lay it down on its side and wait for the mouse to go in to chow down, and then I'll snap the lid back on.

He grabbed the jar and made his way back to the refrigerator door. He opened the jar, held the lid in the same hand he had grabbed the refrigerator door handle with, and slowly swung the fridge open. He looked carefully around the interior for a minute or two and settled on a spot for his peanut butter snare. He was just about to lay the jar on its side when his mouth fell open, and his eyes stretched beyond his sockets at the drama on one of the shelves. A big stainless steel pot jumped and bounced into various and sundry food items while its lid clinked and clanked up and down as though something inside the pot was hankering to get out.

Whoa!

He slammed the door shut and stepped back from the fridge in utter disbelief.

If that was a mouse in there, it had to have been on steroids. That had to have been a rat in the pot. No doubt about it. There must be a hole in the back of the refrigerator. That's how it got in there.

He walked quickly into his bedroom, reached into the drawer of his nightstand, grabbed his loaded thirty eight-caliber-pistol, and returned to the kitchen.

I'm gonna kill that damn thing, whatever it is. I'm not havin' critters in my refrigerator.

An ounce of caution prevailed. He decided to call his best friend before annihilating the thing in the pot.

"Hey Aaron, this is Marshall. You won't believe this man, but I got a rat in my refrigerator, inside a big pot."

"What? Git outa here, man. A rat in your refrigerator? How do you know it's a rat?"

"What else could it be? I mean the pot is jumpin' and bouncin' around on the shelf, and the lid is clinkin' up and down, and it's a big pot, man. It has to be somethin' as big as a rat."

"So, what did it do, climb in the pot and pull the lid over top of it? If it is a rat, it wouldn't be stuck in a pot. Dude, them things are strong as hell. It would be runnin' around your refrigerator, eatin' everything in sight."

"Well, whatever it is, it'll be dead in a minute. I got my thirty-eight, and I'm gonna kill it and the pot,"

Marshall released the pistol's safety lock.

"Whoa, hey wait a minute man. You can't shoot up your refrigerator homie. That's crazy. What if the bullet ricochets? You could kill the pot, the thing, and yourself. Anyway, it's illegal to discharge a firearm in your apartment. What are you gonna tell the police? You were actin' in self-defense, that you were comin around the corner, and your refrigerator jumped you?"

Marshall stopped to consider what Aaron was telling him. Their conversation continued, including a discussion of what else could be in the pot. Marshall recalled making one of his taste sensations six months ago, that consisted of just about everything in the refrigerator that was about to spoil, and boiling it for a half hour or more before having it for dinner. Afterward, when the pot cooled down, he shoved it into the refrigerator and hadn't opened it since.

"Hey, remind me not to eat anything at your crib," Aaron said. "That's not a rat in your refrigerator. It's one of them damn taste sensations that's grown into some kind of bacteria-mold-thing, and it's tryin' to get out of that pot."

Aaron was well aware of the creative history of Marshall's taste sensations. At times he would combine so many condiments on a sandwich, that sometimes the burger, or turkey, or whatever the main ingredient happened to be, would become indistinguishable from the piled-on additives. Spaghetti was often another conglomeration of any and all things edible, and it went by the name whatever.

Aaron convinced Marshall to get some duct tape and seal the lid on the pot and take it somewhere to throw it away. After struggling with the bouncing pot, Marshall sealed it and placed it in a bag and carried it outside to his car. He put the bag in the trunk and drove off to find a spot to toss it. The noise from the trunk was a little scary. It kept getting louder and sounded like the bag was rolling around in the trunk. Marshall was crossing the bridge leading into town. He couldn't stand the noise any longer, and the fear grew in his mind that whatever was in the pot might break free and find a home in his car. He pulled over, opened the trunk, grabbed the bag, and gave it a toss over the rail and into the fast-moving current of the Mississippi River.

Whew. I'm goin' home and clean out my refrigerator, and vow never to keep anything in it longer than a week.

Several months went by, and Marshall had stuck to his vow. He cleaned out his refrigerator and never let food stay in it longer than a week before eating or tossing it out. He did not want to relive the strange pot thing episode that happened in his kitchen. He had turned over a new leaf. Then one evening as he climbed into bed, his phone rang. He debated with himself over answering it and finally decided to pick up the phone on his nightstand.

"Hello, this is Marshall."

"Hello, sir, we have a collect call for you from New Orleans."

"What, I don't know anybody in New Orleans."

"Sir, will you accept the charges?"

"Okay, I guess."

"Hello, this is Marshall. Who is this?"

"Clink, clack, clinkity, thump."

What the?

Marshall dropped the phone and reached for his pistol.

It couldn't be. No way. The refrigerator thing is not only still alive, it called me on the telephone?

He stepped away from the bed and was shocked when he saw a strange little hairy green leg with a mangled foot and three gnarled toes stepping out of the phone. He fired three shots from his pistol at the emerging creature, and as he backed away, stepped on the base of his vacuum cleaner. He slipped and fell, hitting his head on the corner of his dresser and was knocked unconscious.

Marshall awakened but was back in his bed. His phone rang, and as he looked around the bedroom, everything seemed normal. There was nothing out of place, and there was no little creature to be found.

"Hey, this is Marshall."

"Marshall, this is Aaron. I thought you were gonna meet us at the gym for our Saturday morning hoops. What happened to you?"

"Man, I had this crazy dream and must have overslept. I know one thing. I'll never eat another one of my taste sensations right before I go to bed."

"That sounds like a plan. Well, hey, we're gonna head over to the deli on Fourth for some grub. Get your lazy ass outa bed, and join us."

"Okay, I'll be there in a few."

Marshall hung up the phone and swung his feet out of bed but sudden pain from the back of his head gave him pause. He put his hand on the spot it was coming from, and there to his surprise was a large knot.

That's it. I'll never even make another taste sensation again, let alone eat one.

Average Ordinary Harry

If you had never been introduced to Harry, you certainly wouldn't take note of him if you passed him on the sidewalk or stood next to him on an elevator. Even those of us who knew Harry well and lived in close proximity to his crib in the hood had trouble distinguishing him from anyone else in the city. He was just that ordinary, common, average, with little or no unique characteristics. He was quiet, never drew attention to himself, and rarely wore any color other than drab. Unobtrusive, unremarkable, and inconspicuous were all operative definitions. That's why we called him Average Ordinary Harry.

I remember one Friday afternoon how his brother, Ed, asked a bunch of us standing on the corner if we had seen Harry. Not only could we not recall seeing him that day, but neither of us could bring to mind the last time we had seen him. It was like asking someone to recall the thirty-seventh raindrop that fell on their car windshield in a sudden downpour. Ed's description of him didn't help either.

"You know he's not too tall and not too short and had on a pair of pants and a shirt."

That left all of us scratching our heads and furrowing our brows as we searched for clues amongst a vapid area of memory related to the often obscure exploits of Average Ordinary Harry.

"What, are you kiddin' me?" I asked. "A pair of pants and a shirt? Look around man. Every dude out here is wearin' a pair of pants and a shirt."

And Ed pointed out, "Hey, there's a guy with a sweater on."

"Okay, well, yeah, we'll all look real hard for him," I said, as my friends and I turned to walk in the other direction. We all knew it was pointless to look for Harry. You were apt to miss him in a photograph, even if you were looking at it through a magnifying glass. Rumor has it that when Harry was five years old, he and his mother were walking past a department store downtown, and she turned to look at a dress on a mannequin in the window. She took her eye off of Harry for an instant, and he disappeared. The ensuing hunt for him was frantic, and everyone within earshot and eyesight of his mother had been mustered into the search party. They looked everywhere and anywhere, still no Harry. At her wit's end, his mother leaned her head against the department store window and there, on the other side of the window, on the floor next to a mannequin, sat Harry, waving to his mother with an innocent wry little smile on his face. He had been sitting there for an hour and a half, unnoticed by everyone who had been looking for him. He just seemed to blend in with the mannequins.

I smiled at the recollection of Harry's childhood downtown disappearance as my friends, and I walked for several blocks through the scattered orange, red, and brown leaves strewn here and there until we parted at the intersection of Frankstown and Homewood Avenues. I turned the corner and continued alone down the many broken, and disheveled concrete sidewalk blocks headed toward

Mr. D's greasy spoon restaurant. I was already tasting the gumbo they had become famous for all over the city. And then, strangely, as though he had been there all the time, Average Ordinary Harry was strolling alongside of me.

"Hey man, where did you come from?" I asked. "Your brother is lookin' for you."

Harry just smiled and nodded his head as he quickened his pace and soon stepped away from my side. He could be odd that way. If there was ever anyone who believed in the adage of giving everyone your ear but few your voice, it was Harry. He was so quiet and unnoticeable that I tried to imagine what he could possibly do for a living, and then it hit me. Harry was a spy, working for the CIA. That had to be it. He would be perfect for the job. I could see him moving stealthily among the darkly framed buildings and streets of a major city in some foreign country on assignment.

I imagined him leaning out of the shadows with a black patch over one eye and wearing a trench coat with the collar pulled up around his neck, and of course, he'd have a fierce black hat on his head with the brim tilted toward the floor. I could see a beautiful woman, a dangerous double-agent, no doubt, waiting for him to join her at a table in a small café, hatching a nefarious plot to seduce him and drug him so she could steal the secrets he carried in the hidden pocket of his trench coat. But then I realized that Harry was too bland to wear anything fierce. A black hat and a black patch over his eye and a trench coat just weren't his style of drab. It would be more normal for him to dress like the most boring and ordinary local folks. That was his trademark here, and he would be just as unassuming everywhere else. That made even more sense. He would blend in with his new surroundings. I could still imagine the double agent, however, but she would be plain, unobtrusive, wearing a bun hairstyle and glasses.

I became intrigued with the idea of finding out what Average Ordinary Harry did for a living. But how on earth could I uncover the secret world of the only human chameleon I've ever known, who could be hiding some deep dark secret, something that motivated his clandestine existence? After all, Harry and his kin lived in an Addams Family type house, partly secluded by huge bushes and scraggly trees on a strange little street that ended at the beginning of their driveway. That thought, although a little disconcerting, made me all the more eager to discover the truth.

I decided to begin by casually asking a few questions about Harry around the neighborhood, an activity that left most scratching their heads and asking, "Who?" All except for Raefield Smith, the rotund and robust cook at Mr. D's restaurant. He was known for having his ear to the ground, and for being in possession of at least a little bit of information about everything and anything in the community. Once inside the restaurant, I sidled up to the end of the counter closest to the kitchen and yelled back to Raefield.

"Hey Raefield, I need to borrow some information from you, man. I'll pay it back with interest."

That got his attention, and he walked toward me carrying the biggest spatula I've ever seen.

"Damn, man, what the hell could you be cookin with that big ass spatula?" I questioned.

"Big ass burgers," he replied. "What else?"

I began to tell him of my quest to find out where Ordinary Harry worked.

"I can only tell you what I've heard. He may have worked, about a year ago, at the candle and incense store down on Hamilton Avenue. I don't know what he did there, but I heard someone say they saw him coming out of the backroom one day with an apron on."

"Okay, I've always liked the incense they sell. I think I'll stop by there later today."

"Let me give you some advice, man. I wouldn't go in there askin' questions. Everybody who works there is kind of strange: especially the chick who works at the counter. She has a mustache, and I don't mean a thin line. It's thick enough for dreadlocks, and she only has three teeth in her mouth, right up front. So don't say anything to make her laugh, but if you do, you better laugh with her and not at her. The last person to laugh at her was Silly Sam. I heard she secretly sprinkled some powder on the incense he bought. He got home and lit the incense to freshen up the stale air in his front room. About an hour later, he started coughin', and for three weeks, he coughed up little white bird feathers."

"Come on, man; you're bullshittin' me."

"I'm only serious man, beware of those who practice the secret arts. You know you can buy a bag of powders, or a mojo hand, or some John the Conqueror Root, or a spell or two down there. Just be respectful, and you'll be cool."

I thanked Raefield for the information, and after downing a huge bowl of gumbo left the restaurant headed for home. The wind had picked up and began swirling leaves and a cooler temperature around me as I mulled over the idea of stopping by the candle and incense shop on my way home. Hovering, deep, pale blue twilight drew me in, gave me pause, and filtered everything in its grasp. I walked slowly, thinking, wandering through the drowsy evening drift hanging over the city and found myself standing in front of the window of the Full Moon Incense and Candle Shop. A beckoning finger signaled to me. I turned the ornate wooden doorknob and felt its intricately carved figures leave their impression on the palm of my hand.

Once inside, aromatic jasmine, lilac, lemon, and rose incense overwhelmed my nostrils. My eyes filled with a rainbow of candles in various and sundry sizes and shapes that were stacked from the floor to the ceiling on shelves running the full length of the back wall of the shop. Then the rest of the body belonging to the finger that beckoned my entry to the shop appeared directly in front of me. I immediately recognized her from Raefield's description. The thick mustache was unmistakable, and so were the scant teeth in her mouth, but I had no desire to laugh. Her demeanor was sweet, and for some reason, I felt very comfortable in her presence.

"What can I help you with baby?" she asked.

"I want some incense, but you have so much, I don't know what to choose."

"Take your time sugar. If you need some help, holla," she said as she squeezed my arm and walked back behind the counter. As I meandered around the shop, I noticed several people exiting the back room of the shop wearing aprons and carrying candles.

"How many people do you have working here?" I asked.

"They don't work here. They were makin' their own candles in our back room. If you ever want to make a candle or your own brand of incense, we can show you how in our back workshop, for a small fee. I might even waive the fee for you, sugar."

I smiled and said, "I'll keep that in mind," as I grabbed a pack of lemon incense and walked over to the cash register, paid my bill and walked toward the door.

"Thanks. I might come back and make a candle."

"Anytime, honey. Just ask for Nona."

I grabbed and turned the inside doorknob, which felt very warm, and I had trouble letting go. It clung to the palm of my hand for several intense seconds. I had to grab the door with my other hand and forcefully yank my hand from the knob. Freeing my hand, I glanced back at Nona, who was smiling and winking at me.

"Remind me to never cross that threshold again," I said to myself and waved goodbye as I quickly stepped away from the shop. Fifteen minutes later I stood in front of my apartment building, faced with a decision. Should I take the incense I had bought inside, or should I walk around the side of the building and toss it in the trash? I had visions of little white bird feathers exiting my mouth and of my wandering trance-like into the arms of Nona again and again.

"Nothing but net," I exclaimed as the incense arched into the empty dumpster. Inside my apartment and warm, I ended the day by falling asleep in front of the television, and it was three o'clock in the morning when I finally dragged off to bed. Saturday crept lazily up the side of my face as I snored late into the morning. I gradually fell out of bed, showered, and jumped down the apartment steps, and quickly walked to the repair shop to pick up my car. I had been looking forward to this day for weeks. My girlfriend, Nadette, was due back in town and I was going to pick her up at the airport in the evening. We were to have dinner together and spend the rest of the night catching up on lost romantic interludes.

Nadette and I had clicked instantly. We met when she was standing in line at the license bureau, waiting to pick up tabs for her car when she dropped her paperwork. I was standing in back of her, and immediately bent down to help her gather her documents. She also stooped to pick them up, and we looked into each other's eyes. She smiled and stole my heart as I felt the room brighten from the glow of her pearly white teeth. I thought she was the prettiest thing I had ever seen and wasted no time in introducing myself and asking her for a date. She playfully accepted my invitation and wrote her telephone number on my forehead. I whipped out my cell phone, took a picture of my face, and she wiped her number from my forehead. That's when I knew it was kismet. With me being somewhat of a germophobe, it was extraordinary that I let her use a tissue that she had moistened with saliva. I had no objections. She had the softest hands you can imagine, and their silky smooth presence on my face was like a bonding agent.

I had a little extra time, so I decided to spend it with my buddies at the poolroom before heading to the airport. Inadvertently I drove past the candle shop on the way to the pool room and had stopped at the red light just beyond the shop. I glanced back and swore I saw Nona, standing in the doorway waving at me. Still more interestingly, I saw someone who looked like Harry strolling across the threshold.

"Could he really work there?" I asked myself. I was certainly not about to follow him into the shop, but decided to circle the block and park far enough away to be hidden from view. From my vantage point, I could see the front door of the shop and all who entered and left it. I felt like I was doing some real reconnoitering until Harry walked past my car and waved to me. Then I felt a little sheepish and stupid as I waved back and started my engine. At least it wasn't Nona. But who was it I saw entering the shop? Then I remembered that anybody could be mistaken for Harry. That was part of his modus operandi.

I struggled with my curiosity. Maybe the best thing to do was to simply ask him what he did for a living. But then I might have to explain why I wanted to know, and that would be a question I couldn't answer. Perhaps it was a consequence of Harry's ordinariness. Could anyone remain so average and ordinary all his or her life? What business was it of mine what he did for a living anyway? Could he have heard that I had been asking questions about him in the neighborhood? Maybe it was best to leave the man to his own devices and stop intruding on his personal space.

I decided to table my quest, at least temporarily. I had only time enough to get to the airport to pick up my honey. I arrived in the parking garage and walked through the automatic doors into the cavernous terminal and strolled close to the security gate. I had figured on waiting there for my girlfriend to exit the other side of the gate. People gradually walked past where I was standing and deposited their belongings on the conveyor belt to be scanned. My attention was drawn to the vastly different types and colors of shoes that folks were wearing. Most of them had at least one shared reality; they were easy to remove and slip back into, and tie-ups were greatly outnumbered. While my attention was focused on shoes and feet, another person of interest floated past my field of vision.

It was Average Ordinary Harry. He walked briskly to the gate and was waved through security without hesitation.

"What the?" I thought. "How could that happen?"
When he passed through the gate, he turned and winked, allowing me to see a trench coat over his arm and a fierce black hat in his hand. There was a beautiful woman trailing behind him, adjusting her sunglasses and looking over her shoulder, and behind her was a familiar mustache over scant teeth and under another fierce black hat heading for the gate.

"Hi sugar," she said.

I thought it too unbelievable, but before I could digest what had happened, Nadette, the light of my life, entered the room, and nothing else seemed important. The day's activities gave me much to tell her that night. For the moment, all that was ordinary and average and common had been overshadowed by Nadette's glow, and all was right and extraordinary in my world.

The Snake that Ate Summer

Oh, snap! If I don't find Rufus before he slithers his way into my mother's reception, she'll cancel my fifteenth birthday. I'll stay fourteen for the rest of my life and be banished to the basement forever. Where does a six-foot python go in three minutes?

I see a strangely familiar grey-and brown streak out of the corner of my eye.

Wait, it's him slidin' through the dining room window.

I make it to the window in time to grab hold of his tail.

Damn, he's strong as hell.

I tug and tug, but he must be wrapped around somethin' inside because I can't budge him an inch backward. I can't let go. If I do he'll make everybody in the dining room go berserk. The people in this reception are important clients of my parent's restaurant business. Most of them have never even seen the black part of the city or been at a reception in the hood and none of them have ever been inside my crib before.

Rufus ends up bein' too strong, and slippery for me to hold onto and slides out of my grasp. I hoist myself up onto the windowsill in time to see him eyeball a small dog in the hands of Mrs. Gaston, one of the most influential women in the city. Rufus looks intent on makin' the dining room his afternoon café. He glides along the back wall measurin' the speed and accuracy needed to snatch the small Pomeranian Mrs. Gaston is affectionately holdin' in her lap. My eyeballs pop out of my head when I see the Pomeranian gettin' agitated, sensin' the presence of something very dangerous. Its ears perk up, and the nervous pooch begins barkin' and tryin' to jump down onto the floor.

"Hey! Pomee. What's the matter girl? Everything's okay," Mrs. Gaston says.

"Mommy's here. What's the matter, baby?"

Now I'm freakin' out, as I see the dog bite its master and leap from her hand onto the dining room table and straight into the bowl of potato salad.

Oh, that's perfect. Make yourself even more appetizin'. Smell like a salad-dipped morsel for Rufus to munch on.

Mrs. Gaston gasps and rushes toward the table just as Rufus is raisin' his head on the other side. He looks hungry. It is as though time stands still for a few seconds at least. Mrs. Gaston does. She freezes like water at thirty-two below zero. The expression on her face is one of fear and disbelief as the only thing movin' is the pee runnin' down her leg. Then she faints and falls over on top of the Pomeranian, the potato salad bowl, and the dining room table.

It's the best thing she could have done to keep Rufus from snatchin' her dog and puttin' the squeeze on it before swallowin' it whole. But it's not so good after all because she pushes her dog further down into the salad bowl.

Everyone in the room is now aware of my six-foot Python as they bolt from the dining room like the space shuttle blastin' off from Cape Canaveral. People are bumpin' into each other tryin' to find the fastest way out of the dining room. It's like the running of the bulls in that town in Spain. It's everyone for themselves, and it's dangerous. Now I'm afraid for Rufus, because of all the panic and what he might do. He could freak out and wrap himself around one of these rich folks and hold on for dear life. I have to save Rufus and anyone who might get too close to him. In through the window I go and down on to the floor.

"Rufus! Come here Rufus!"

The scene is right out of a bizarre Godzilla movie. Rufus is tryin' to dislodge Mrs. Gaston from the top of the potato salad bowl and her Pomeranian. I grab him by the back and begin to pull him away from Mrs. Gaston. He's not happy and wraps himself around my arm and begins to squeeze.

"I'm not goin for it, Rufus. You don't scare me."

I squeeze him and begin to walk out of the all but empty dining room. Just then, my dad steps into the room with one of the worst looks I've ever seen on his face. It's one of disgust and disappointment with me and concern for Mrs. Gaston. She is still sprawled over the potato salad bowl like a huge garnish.

"Son, what did you let happen?" he says, rushin' to Mrs. Gaston's aid. "All you had to do was keep that damn snake in the basement for another half-hour and the reception would have been over."

"It wasn't my fault, Dad. You know Rufus. He's an escape artist. I locked the cage and locked the basement door. I still don't know how he got out. There must be a hole down there somewhere. He found a way to get out of the cage and slither through the wall somehow."

"Billy, those are excuses. You should have stayed with Rufus to ensure that nothing would go wrong. You didn't want to join us at the luncheon, so there was no acceptable reason for not watching Rufus."

People are now jumpin' into cars and burnin' rubber in our driveway like they had gotten the checker flag at the Indianapolis 500. Things are crazy now, and our house and everything in a half-mile radius is in chaos. Meanwhile, back in the dining room, my dad is liftin' Mrs. Gaston off of the table. He sits her down in the only chair still upright on the entire first floor. She is covered in potato salad and looks like she was on the losin' side of a massive food fight. I have Rufus under control on my arm and can't believe my eyes at the spectacle on the dining room table.

The only thing visible of the Pomeranian is the tail, and it's not movin', nor is any other part of it. The dog is suspended motionless in the potato salad bowl. Mrs. Gaston, coming out of her faint, sees this and jumps up from the chair and rushes over to the table. She sticks her hands down into the bowl and retrieves the limp body of her once hyperactive little pooch and begins to shake it.

"Pomee, Pomee, speak to me Pomee."

It's no use; the dog is gone. It suffered a horrible fate, smothered in a bowl of gourmet potato salad by its owner. Its last moments were spent inhalin' relish and eggs and mustard and onions, while it did the breaststroke in a gooey but tasty recipe fit for the city's finest residents.

The dog, our house, and the future of the business deal my parents wanted are all a mess. I don't even want to think of what my mother will say, so I sneak off to hide in the basement. It is the only quiet and peaceful place on the block. I know our neighbors are shakin' their heads and suckin' their teeth, and talkin' about me and Rufus. They're makin' bets on which one of us is gonna be put out of the house. I'm the odds-on favorite.

This is not the first time my snake has gotten me into trouble. A week after school was out for the summer, Rufus escaped the basement and hid in the bushes between our house and the next-door neighbors' house and caught their cat and ate it. Two weeks after that, he almost gave the mailman a heart attack after he got out again and slid off of the porch roof onto his back as he was tryin' to deliver our mail. In the middle of this summer, he got out of his cage again and somehow slithered into an ice cream truck as it was parked on the sidewalk, waitin' for customers. Just when a bunch of little kids were at the window tryin to decide what they wanted, Rufus raised his head up next to the server and stuck out his tongue. The kids screamed and bolted down the sidewalk and the server jumped out of the window and ran past them.

When I get down in the basement, I see that I did lock Rufus in his cage, but the door is twisted open. So that's how he did it. He is so much stronger than we all realize. He pushed his way between the hinges and bent the wire out of shape. Now my parents are all bent out of shape because of their dough head son and his snake. I would run away, but I'm sure Rufus would find me and screw things up for me where ever I go. I guess I can't blame him. It's his nature. I bet he smelled or somehow sensed that little dog upstairs and thought it was the dinner bell bein' rung. He was only answering the call of nature, which reminds me, I know I'll be the one who'll have to clean up Mrs. Gaston's pee from the dining room carpet. That'll just be one of my punishments. They might even rub my nose in it like we used to do to our first puppy to keep him from peein' inside again.

As I fall into the old chair in the basement, I think about just lettin' Rufus go, send him off on his own. I should let him fend for himself, except I think he would just eat what he could of the neighbor's pets and then come back here pickin' his teeth with their bones. I could have him stuffed and mounted on a post, or have him skinned and make a pair of boots or a belt or a couple of wallets out of him.

I look over at him in his cage, and he just looks like the picture of innocence. I think he can sense my frustration. He probably is thinkin' that it's us who are to blame. We have no business havin' a pet python anyway. It was me who convinced my parents to let me have him when he was a harmless little thing. I'm the only child my parent's have. My baby sister died soon after she was born, and the doctors told my mother she wouldn't be able to have any more children. My parents spoil me, but I try to be a good son, and I swore I would take good care of Rufus so they wouldn't have to worry about him. I know now that he would be much happier at home in the wild, catchin', and eatin' things like he tried to do this afternoon. Just then, I hear a siren outside. I hope no one else got hurt. It would be just my luck for someone to have gotten into an accident racin' away from the afternoon's craziness in our house. Well, soon I'll be eighteen, and I'll be off to college. I just have to make it through the next few years with my folks and Rufus. At least I know I won't be takin' him to college with me unless he goes as the outside of one of my suitcases.

I push Rufus' cage squarely against the wall and quietly crawl up the basement steps to the side door. As I peek out of the little glass window, I see Mrs. Gaston being raised into an ambulance. She's still holdin' onto her dead Pomeranian. It is on her stomach like a flower arrangement. My mother is sayin' something to her as she stands at the back of the ambulance and sees me peekin' out of the window. She angrily waves her finger at me, and I duck down below the windowpane.

"Billy," my father yells from the kitchen. "Come up here and help me clean up this mess."

"Okay, Dad. Let me check on Rufus first."

I run back down the steps only to see that the cage door is bent back open and empty again. I can't believe my eyes. I didn't hear a thing. I frantically scour the basement lookin' for him and come upon his escape hatch, a small window on the back wall of the basement that had been sealed shut for years. It is not until I get right up on it that I'm able to see an opening on the bottom corner. I can see little bits of snakeskin left on the edge of the window.

"Billy, what are you doing?" my dad asks as he walks down the steps. He stops at the bottom of the steps when he sees Rufus' empty cage.

"Not again, son, not again. My God boy, we're in the midst of a crisis, and here we go again."

He walks over to the gun cabinet, where he keeps two rifles locked up for safekeeping.

"What are you gonna do Dad?"

"When we find Rufus, I'm going to put him out of his misery."

"You can't Dad. He's just a snake bein a snake. He can't help it."

"And neither can I, son. I'm just a dad being a dad. We not only have to live in this community, we have to make a living here. This afternoon was a disaster. I doubt if we gained any friends willing to help us get the area around the restaurant rezoned so we can expand."

"But it's not Rufus' fault, Dad."

"Look, son, it doesn't matter who or what's at fault anymore. We have to put an end to the disruptions your snake is causing in the neighborhood. He is interfering with our business and our peace of mind."

My father unlocks the gun cabinet and takes out his thirty-thirty rifle.

"I can't believe you're gonna do this Dad. He's just a pet snake."

"Let's go, Billy. It's time for you to grow up."

I can't see my bein' a part of killin' Rufus, and I make my own escape up the steps and out the side door. I run until my sides ache, and I'm doubled over with my hands on my knees trying to catch my breath. I know my parents are gonna be upset with me over all that happened today. They're always tryin' to get me to do the right thing, and I do most of the time, cause I love my parents, but if I can find Rufus first maybe I can give him to the zoo or find someone who'll take care of him.

I look around to see where I am because I've been runnin' blindly without payin' attention to where I was headed. I've arrived at the Highland Park reservoir about a mile and a half from home. I know I have to begin makin' my way back closer to home. I know that a Burmese Python can go about a mile in an hour, if it wants to. Rufus is liable to be hangin' out in a tree somewhere. I start walkin' back toward my house, tryin' to keep an eye out for my father and Rufus. As I get to within a half-mile of my house, I see a crowd of people gathered in front of the public library, and other people are runnin' out of the library like they had seen a ghost. It must be Rufus again!

I carefully walk around to the back of the library because if not huntin' for food, Rufus will be tryin' to avoid people, especially a crowd of nervous people. I'm sure that somebody called the police. Some people in the community have asked my parents to get rid of Rufus. They say they are scared of him now and when he gets bigger, he'll be way too much for me to handle. I reach the back corner of the library and make my way to the center of the building, and I see him. There he is coiled up on the ledge outside of one of the windows on the ground floor. The window is partially open. I guess that's why people left the library in a hurry. I have to get to him and coax him down.

Then what do I do? Where can I go with him? How far can I get with him?

First things first, I have to get him down from the ledge. I find a big rock and roll it directly beneath the window. I stand on top of it and stretch my arm out to the ledge.

"Rufus, come on, boy, come on down."

After a few minutes or so, he warms to the idea of curlin' around my arm, and he crawls up around my shoulder and wraps around my body. I climb down from the rock and slowly make my way to the side of the library. I stop in my tracks because I see my father with his rifle in hand, walkin' up the front steps of the building. At least he hasn't seen me yet, and I crouch down behind a clump of bushes. Out of the corner of my eye, I see a small shed in the back of one of the library's garbage dumpsters. If I can make it over there, maybe I can stash Rufus inside until I can find a safer place for him. Lookin' carefully around, and seein' no one, I inch my way over to the shed. Luckily it's open, and Rufus and I slip inside.

After lookin' for a place to hide Rufus, I slowly push him off of my body, and he coils up on top of an old crate. I open the shed door, slip outside, and slide the door closed again. Around to the front of the library, up the steps and into the first-floor reading section, I make my way to where my father is talkin' to the librarian. I walk over to where the two of them are standin'.

"Billy, you need to go home. Your mother is there. She's worried about you. You need to go home and stay there."

"Okay, Dad," I say without hesitation, knowin' that I've just stashed Rufus in the garage shed. My worry is whether he'll stay there until I can come back and get him. I turn and nervously walk out of the library. I stop to look back to see what people are doin' and where my father just might be headed to in the library. I see a police squad car pull up in front of the library. I knew it was just a matter of time before they would arrive. But then I figure that it might have something to do with my dad carryin' a loaded rifle around town and into the public library. The police get out of their car and rush up the steps. My curiosity gets the best of me and I follow them. To my surprise, when I get back into the library, I see my father with his rifle pointed out of the window toward the shed in back of the dumpster and guess that Rufus has slithered out of where I hid him.

"Sir, drop the weapon," one of the cops says.

My father puts his rifle down and turns around.

"George, what the hell are you doing?" the cop asks my dad.

"Mark, I was just about to end this bizarre snake drama before you guys showed up. My son's snake is coiled up next to that shed in the back."

My father knows these policemen. He served for a long time as a volunteer fireman and got to know a lot of cops that way. Soon they all gather as my dad points out of the window.

"Do you think you can get him from here?" the cop asks.

"I'm positive," my dad says.

I can't believe they're even talkin' about lettin' my father shoot out of the window at Rufus.

"How crazy is that?" I say out loud. I've got to stop this. I run down the steps and race around the back of the building.

"Go, Rufus, Go, Go," I say as I step between him and the sight of my father's rifle.

To my surprise, an animal rescue van drives between the building and Rufus, and two people emerge from both sides of the vehicle. My father can't fire at Rufus, and I run over to where they stopped. I tell them where he is, and together, we get Rufus into one of the cages inside the van. Shortly, my father and the police officers join us in back of the library.

"So, we got a call about a dangerous snake on a ledge of the library, and we came right over," one of the animal rescue team says. We will take him to the zoo if nobody here objects."

"That will be fine," my father says. "What do you think son?"

"I think that will be good dad." I can always go visit Rufus there."

They lock the door Rufus sits behind in a cage and drive off.

My father's phone rings, and he answers it, but it is on speaker mode.

"Hello George, this is William Gaston. I just wanted to let you know that city council approved your zoning request and your application for development funding."

"What? That's great Councilman Gaston. Thank you. I am thrilled."

"Well, you should probably be thanking that snake of yours. The vote was tied, and I hadn't made up my mind yet. Then I got a frantic call from my wife about what happened at your reception. I was sorry her dog died, but that little ankle biter and I were not friendly. I can't tell you how many times it nipped my hands or ankles. I could not convince my wife to get rid of it for all the money in the world. So, when I heard that it went swimming in a bowl of potato salad and drowned, I sighed and voted to approve your applications. I won't have to wear high top leather boots in my own home anymore."

"I'm sorry things got out of hand at my place Councilman Gaston, but it seems like we were both the beneficiaries of the misadventures of my son's snake. By the way, that snake is on its way to the local zoo right now and won't be a problem anymore."

"That's good, George. I hope your son won't miss his snake too much. I know from my wife's attitude toward her little pooch how we can get attached to our pets."

"Thank you. I will find a way to make it up to him."

"Okay, well, goodbye, and good luck."

Together my dad and I walk silently back to our car, relieved that despite everything that went wrong today, it ended right for us, and Rufus is now in the hands of professional animal handlers. I hoped that he will like his new home and that he will stay there and away from the local Pomeranian population.

"Hey Dad, what do you think about an aquarium with Piranha?"

Tangential Dilemma

"I don't believe that. It's impossible," Melvin said.

"Hey, I'm serious, man. It's true," Kirkland replied. "I read it in one of those world record books. Some guy in Colorado cut off a chicken's head, and after about three or four minutes, the body of the chicken tried to peck the ground with its neck. The body of the chicken refused to die. Then the guy decided to see how long he could keep the chicken alive and started dripping liquid food down its gullet. The chicken lived for eighteen months like that before it croaked."

"Man, that's bullshit. I still don't believe you."

"Why would I lie about a damn chicken? Look, go online, and Google longest living chicken with its head cut off, and you'll see."

Melvin, a chronic naysayer, walked over to the computer and searched the internet, as Kirkland had suggested. He pulled up information, verifying his friend's claims.

"Damn, that's still hard to believe. I see what you were saying, and there's even a picture here with the chicken's head on the ground next to its feet."

"Weird, isn't it? But that's what these people who want me to join their organization were talking about. They used it as an example of how the body, any living thing's body, was just a glob of protoplasm and bones and fluid and other miscellaneous biological shit. They were telling me how the chicken's body lived without its head and then they made the leap to their theory that our bodies were also capable of living without our consciousness, that it was possible to separate our conscious minds from our sub-conscious minds and our bodies would go on living and functioning. We would be like a dog or a chicken or some other dumbass living thing, unaware of ourselves. That's fascinating to me, man. I mean like that's what separates us from the animal kingdom, being aware of ourselves. To think that it's possible, in our lifetime, to revert to a state that would make us more like the rest of the animal life in the world is hard to believe. Anyway, these people say that say they know how to make the separation and then make our conscious minds more advanced while housed in a machine that can be continuously upgraded. I want to check it out. They've really piqued my interest."

"So, the body without its conscious mind would revert back to the animal stage like before humans evolved into intelligent creatures, sort of an instant de-evolution? That's freaky."

"I told you, man. These guys call themselves Humachs and they're having a meeting next week. You gotta come to the meeting with me. I need someone with me, especially someone like you who doesn't believe in anything, someone who is hard to convince."

Melvin agreed to attend the next Humachs meeting in Highland Square with Kirkland, and the two of them decided to talk a day or so before the meeting was to be held. Melvin, a high school math teacher in the heart of the roughest black community, was an extremely pessimistic, but rational individual and rarely participated in extraneous endeavors. He was on a straight and narrow path toward the attainment of several goals he had made for himself and never wavered. He was in grad school and had been trying to build an organization to help struggling high school students strengthen their math and science skills. Kirkland, on the other hand, a gifted and talented jazz musician, was all over the place. He was quick to investigate the latest quirky thing, and spent a lot of time searching for new Nirvanas, new horizons. This one, however, promised to be more fascinating than anything he had ever become involved in.

Kirkland continued reading information circulating in the city about a new organization of people who were advocating the merging of humans with computers. They talked of a new species of living organisms, part human and part machine. He had taped a copy of one of their flyers to the front of his refrigerator, and every time he entered his kitchen he walked over to the refrigerator door and read the notice.

HUMACH SYNERGIES

Come, Let Us Change The Universe

Join The Future Today

Friday December 21

Highland Park Towers 1717 Newland Avenue

MAKE TODAY THE FIRST DAY OF YOUR NEW AND LONGER LIFE. JOIN THE MOST DYNAMIC AND IMPORTANT MOVEMENT EVER TO GRACE THE EARTH. REBEL AGAINST THE FORCES AND ENTITIES THAT CONTROL YOUR CONSCIOUS MIND. ATTEND OUR MEETING AND WE WILL HELP YOU RISE TO A REPRESENTATION OF YOUR HIGHER SELF. FREE THE REAL YOU.

Time jumped by, and Melvin and Kirkland were on their way to the Humachs' meeting. Kirkland's car sliced through the deep twilight that hung like gray dishwater over the city. Glistening streets from recently fallen rain formed a pathway guiding them. Nearing the building housing the meeting, the two men decided to park about a block away, a distance they thought might allow them to gauge what was going on immediately outside of the building. About a half -block away they saw large portable generators operating with huge bundles of wire running from the bottom cabinet to the front door of the entrance to the building they were headed to. Several large men were guarding the generators as if they were valuable property.

Once inside the great hall where the assembly was to take place, Melvin and Kirkland looked for seats. Melvin wanted to sit near the back of the room in case the meeting was boring, but Kirkland wanted a close-up view of everything. Melvin gave in to Kirkland's wish to be in the front of the room, and they were seated in the third row near the aisle. The room filled up quickly, and the crowd of interested people grew to almost standing room capacity. The lights flicked on and off to signal the start of the meeting, and a well-dressed gentleman walked to the center of the stage and began to speak.

"My friends," he said. "Thank you all for coming. Soon you will thank us for bringing you to the most important and greatest reality on earth. Together we will change the world and assume our rightful place in true dominion over the planet. We must free ourselves from the trillions of microorganisms that we host in our bodies that are eating us alive from the inside out. We must free our conscious minds from the struggle with the evil and domineering sub-conscious giant that controls the interior of the sack of meat and bones and fluid we call our bodies.

My friends, you must understand that our conscious minds are a by-product of the evolution of the organism we occupy. It was an accident."

"Whoa, this dude is intense," Melvin said to Kirkland.

"You ain't never lied," Kirkland replied, as he covered his mouth with his hand in an attempt to conceal the fact that he was talking.

The speaker continued with his address after pausing to notice the verbal distraction Melvin and Kirkland had created.

"There will come a time in the next two decades when humans will no longer be able to repair or program computers," he said. "Right now, computer scientists are writing codes that will enable computers to rewrite their programs and become self-sufficient. We will either be ignored as worthless biological units or attacked by machines because we are a detriment to the new mechanical order and ourselves. This is our time to unite with them, to integrate with the machines, to physically link with them, and continue to dominate. We have learned how to download our conscious minds into customized, superior machines that we can repair and upgrade. We will gain immortality. Do you want to live for a thousand years? Come join our cause. Leap across time with us to the dawn of a new species."

The audience rose to its feet and gave the speaker a round of rousing applause. Committed members of the organization moved among the people handing out information flyers and applications for membership. They also paused to answer questions and proselytize with individual attendees.

"This is wild," Kirkland said. "I want to find out more. The idea of becoming a new species is okay, but living for a thousand years is right up my alley. I still have a lot of questions though."

One of the organization's members handed Kirkland papers containing contact information, including dates and times for future meetings and the location of their headquarters.

"Hey man, I hope you're not serious about this bullshit," Melvin said. "Even if they could download your consciousness into a machine, why would you want to do some crazy shit like that? Anyway, you don't know these people. How do you know you can trust them? You can't go to the Better Business Bureau to check them out." You want to become a damn machine, a thing, you want to become a eunuch? Why don't you just donate your balls to science and keep your body?

"Okay, that's funny man, but there might really be something to this new species thing. I remember when the group Parliament Funkadelic was singing, 'Free your mind and your ass will follow.' This is free your mind and forget your ass."

"You need to forget this shit, man, and return to the rational world, where people live and die."

"I'm just gonna see what this is all about, man," Melvin said. "I'm curious, that's all."

"Okay, man. Don't invite me. You better watch your back if you get involved with these people. They look like they're salivating over the prospect of new experimental subjects."

"That's why I need you to come with me," Melvin says.

"From now on my name is Bennett and I ain't in it. Don't call me."

Melvin and Kirkland left the meeting at odds over their impressions of what took place and what the future might bring, according to the Humachs. Kirkland's curiosity had been stoked, and he was intent on finding out where this new idea could take him. Could he really become immortal? He relished the thought of living in the distant future and not just imagining what it would be like. Space travel and discovering life on another planet could be things he could actually experience. He dropped Melvin off at his apartment and continued on home, contemplating the involvement in what he thought could be an exciting new adventure. Perhaps he might even be able to design the kind of machine his conscious mind could exist in.

Later, at home and in bed, Kirkland drifted in and out of sleep and talked through his dreams.

"I need some excitement, something to look forward to, beyond the boring humdrum existence I have now."

It was late in the evening of a common and uneventful Saturday. Even the weather was drab and in a holding pattern over the city. Straight-line winds at around three miles per hour could hardly be called breezes, and low flying insects flitted about effortlessly. Bored and unable to find satisfying entertainment,

Kirkland decided abruptly to visit the place where he had encountered the

Humachs. He walked through two huge metal double doors and immediately into

a buzz of noise and activity. He was immediately told by someone standing near

the front desk of the offices that a visitor from Cleveland, Ohio, who had

witnessed a successful transfer of human intelligence into a machine, was in the

building. Kirkland followed the activity into an interior space that was unlike

anything he had ever witnessed.

Protruding from the walls at varying angles and degrees, were metal pipes and

plastic tubes amid banks of monitors and electronic gadgetry, and blinking multi-

colored lights. The middle of the room was home to large gurneys with adjustable

metal legs, and small teak and mahogany wooden chairs stacked to the ceiling.

Wall shelving contained egg-shaped dark blue and green glass bottles filled with

overflowing white foam that were connected to clear plastic tubing running into

small square metal boxes. Large light fixtures on accordion-like overhangs

beamed focused yellow light onto the floor. Four individuals with flowing white

lab coats pushed the gurneys into positions perpendicular to the walls, while two

others quickly inserted power cords into floor outlets and adjusted the heights of

table legs. Several containers, which were placed on the tables, began to bubble as

a white mist descended from the ceiling.

Kirkland began to feel dizzy. He reached for the wall to steady himself, but the

wall panel he was aiming for retracted as his hand approached. He fell to the floor in a dozing heap and was soon placed on one of the room's large tables. While a gargantuan bearded man in a hospital gown with two blinking red lights on his forehead held Kirkland down, two lab assistants secured him to the table with straps and wheeled him into a pristine and starkly bare anteroom.

"Hey, Kirkland, this is Melvin. Where are you, man? I'm here at the club. I thought you were gonna meet me here?" Melvin left his message on Kirkland's voice mail with urgency. He had been waiting for over an hour. Several days passed, and no one had seen or heard from Kirkland.

"Bro, are you hiding? I've been trying to reach you for a week," Melvin said, leaving his fifth message on Kirkland's phone.

"Where in the hell is this dude?" Melvin said out loud. "He just vanished. I wonder if it has anything to do with those sci-fi creeps he was so interested in?"

Melvin decided to go back to the building where he and Kirkland had attended the Humachs' meeting, but he took several precautions. He slid his thirty eight-caliber-revolver into his back pocket and informed several other friends where and when he was going to visit the organization's facilities. He took a wrestler friend, Big Monte, with him. Monte, six-feet-nine inches tall and weighing a little over three hundred pounds, was a formidable asset. Melvin also informed a friend of his, Detective Harold Foster of the police department, that they were going to look for Kirkland. When Detective Foster agreed to meet them, Melvin decided to leave his pistol home. Good fortune prevailed. A skeleton crew of workers was maintaining the building when they got there, and little resistance was offered, particularly when Foster flashed his badge. Once inside the interior space, they searched every room looking for Kirkland until they reached a locked black metal door with large text written in Latin spawning the door's framework.

"Enter at your own risk," Melvin interpreted, and Detective Foster withdrew his pistol from his holster. The door was locked until Big Monte forcefully applied his girth, and it gave way with sparks flying. The room was bathed in low orange light with strips of various colored Christmas tree lights circling the ceiling's border. There was a figure lying on a gurney, grunting, and struggling to get free. Behind the figure lay a black and red box with flashing orbiting white lights. Melvin rushed over to the gurney and discovered Kirkland fighting to free himself.

"Kirk, hey Kirk, it's me, Melvin."
Kirkland showed no reaction except for continued grunting and struggling to get free of the straps. Melvin continued to talk to Kirkland as he worked to release him from the gurney but large metal screws tightened down the straps, and he could not loosen them.

"Hey, Melvin, hey man, over here.

Melvin walked over to where the sound was coming from and looked over at a shelf where a black and red box was sitting.

"Oh, my God. No, it couldn't be. I don't believe it," Melvin said.

"Yeah, man, it's me. I'm here. They did this to me, man. They drugged me and snatched my consciousness from my body and put it in this box. I'm connected to all this shit in here. I can't see you, but I can hear you, and I can speak."

Detective Foster, Big Monte, and Melvin struggled out the front door with Melvin's disembodied mind and his grunting body as the skeleton crew working at the facility watched. Kirkland's body resisted their attempts to put it in the car and took off running down the sidewalk, wildly flailing its arms. Big Monte chased after Kirkland's body, and when he caught up to it, wrestled it to the ground and hit it in the head with a blackjack knocking it out. Melvin arrived with the car, and the two of them shoved the body into the car and drove back to Kirkland's home. Melvin stepped out of the car and opened the rear door to help Big Monte unload the body from the back seat, when it suddenly attacked him and took off running again. This time it dashed into a nearby alley and vanished. Detective Foster, Big Monte and Melvin searched hours for Kirkland's body to no avail.

Three days later, Foster called Melvin with an update.

"Melvin, this is Harold. I have some news on your buddies' body. It's sitting in a jail cell down at the county. Sheriff's deputies arrested it last night after they were called to a restaurant around ten o'clock. It had crawled into the restaurant and just started taking the food off of people's plates and eating it."

"What? Well, is it okay? Was it injured?"

"It's okay, but things are really strange. Apparently, it acts like a baby. It can't speak, or do any of the things you would expect an adult to do. They are going to transfer it to the psychiatric ward at Bell View."

"Damn, man. That's not good. I just don't think that we'll ever be able to put Kirkland's consciousness and his body back together again."

"The crazy thing about it is that the psychiatrist who examined his body said that in effect, it was like a newborn baby. They have it in a diaper and are feeding it food through a bottle with a nipple on it. They're even trying to teach it how to speak."

"That is what I really didn't want to hear. I talked with a scientist yesterday who said that in a remarkably similar case, where this same organization experimented with another unsuspected and unwilling person, the disenfranchised body began to develop a new consciousness. What will happen if Kirkland's body develops a fully operational second consciousness and becomes self-aware? His former consciousness might be doomed to an existence in that box forever."

"That raises a lot of very difficult questions to answer. Which one will you be most loyal to? If the new consciousness is just like the old one, won't that Kirkland be your buddy? Can two identical conscious minds exist in the same dimension?"

"Those are almost impossible to answer, at least now. I also thought about a more serious question for Kirkland's original conscious mind. Will it be considered alive? Is it like a person with legal rights like other citizens?"

"This is a real dilemma. Where do you begin?"

"I have no idea. The only encouragement I have is what I've heard might be around the bend, technologically speaking. There's talk that the box that Kirkland's original conscious mind is in can be developed so that his mind will be able to see and feel almost like it was in a human body."

"So, he'll in effect be a real live robot."

"Or some derivation, and to think that this all started over some talk about a chicken with its head cut off. But you know, I've been wondering what would happen if Kirkland's body and his conscious mind were brought close together in the same room. Can you help me orchestrate that? I tried to talk to some people at Bell View, but my pleas fell on deaf ears."

"I'm curious about what might happen too. I'll see what I can do.

Detective Foster's connections with the police force helped him arrange to have Kirkland's body brought to an examination room at Bell View Psychiatric Hospital, and he and Melvin arrived with Kirkland's conscious mind in its box. They proceeded directly into a muted white room and observed Kirkland's body sitting in a chair, slumped to one side. Melvin placed Kirkland's boxed consciousness on a small table in the middle of the room.

"So we are here," Kirkland said, and almost immediately, his body sat straight up in the chair. It turned toward the table, stood up and rushed for the box, hoisted it above its head and danced and pranced around the room. It became increasingly more reckless and began running into the walls.

"Whoa. Stop. Stop," Kirkland yelled from the box but his body was uncontrollable. Melvin and Foster rushed toward Kirkland's body but it turned, ran toward the only window in the room, and dove through the glass pane. Kirkland's body crashed to the cement walkway beneath the third-floor examination room window. The box it was holding landed in a group of shrubs several feet away and was unharmed, however, his body was pronounced dead on arrival at the local hospital.

Epilogue

Two Years Later

Life or what passes for life as far as Kirkland is concerned has been challenging but full of cutting-edge scientific developments. The box his conscious mind was initially downloaded into has been upgraded several times. Cameras were installed and connected, giving him 360-degree visibility and auditory controls were improved, allowing him to hear a pin drop in a crowded room. He is still able to speak. Wheels were also installed giving him mobility and the box was made weatherproof, reinforced to withstand shock, and sealed shut with three-inch steel screws.

A number of organizations including the National Science Institutes and Robo Systems are involved with Kirkland and have promised upgrades that will surpass anything he could have done as a human being by leaps and bounds. The state of the art in consciousness transfers has improved greatly as has the understanding of what and how it happens. Many people including senior citizens and those with disabilities have undergone transfers and the waiting list for the procedure grows larger daily.

The legal system is struggling to adapt due to questions about the status of transferred entities and left behind bodies. Attorneys for insurance companies have argued in court that transferees are not people, and the bodies left behind without conscious minds have no identities, and neither is insurable. Civil rights organizations have claimed that new cases of discrimination have evolved, and government agencies have been slow to respond. Legislators are attempting to draft new laws, but so little is known and understood about transferees and their former bodies.

Scientists have discovered that deep in the recesses of the brain, rests a center that can transmit and receive thoughts from other people. Psychiatric medicine has been set back on its heels as psychiatrists have admitted that many of their patients who have reported hearing voices in their brains were actually receiving transmissions from other people. Research has also shown that the conscious human mind exists in certain brain wave frequencies and has a digital address that can be accessed like an internet website. Once the digits are discovered, wireless transmissions to and from the brain's software frequencies can be dialed from remote locations. Scientists have said that humans transmit wireless communications from their brains on a regular basis.

Criminals have taken advantage of the new technology and have learned how to hack into brainwave frequencies of not only transferees but also unsuspecting people who have not undergone the new procedures. They have been able to steal huge amounts of thoughts and ideas from them. Ant-viral computer software companies are designing programs that they say will guard against unwanted mental intrusions. Some people have taken to wearing ceramic bowls over their heads that have been specially designed to prevent access to their brainwave frequencies.

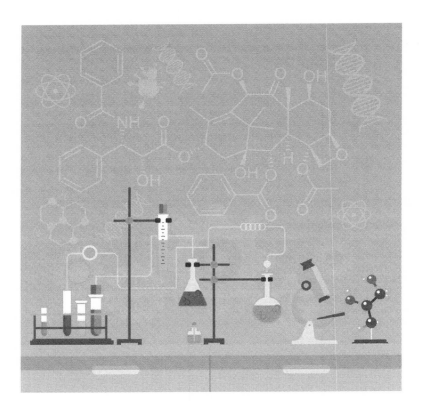

The Dumb Part of the Universe

The sun climbed to its traditionally dominant place in the noonday sky, reining over all beneficiaries of its warmth and light, yet it, like all other things in the low intelligence areas of the universe, obeyed, followed, kowtowed to the physical laws of nature. Carl, a research scientist at West Chemical Laboratories, walked to his office in downtown Cincinnati, enjoying the glow of the summer sun, an acquiescent, dumb ass thing, as defined by the concept laid on him last night by Sasha, a brilliant young scientist at West Labs.

We live in the dumb part of the universe. That's what she said, the dumb part of the universe.

It was hard accepting the idea last night, and he still labored over Sasha's assertions as he strolled to his office. He had read about this idea in science-fiction novels and heard it discussed by an intellectual named Kurzweil, but never thought one of his esteemed colleagues would accept the theory as plausible.

As if we have a choice. As if the sun and moon and stars could just decide to stop behaving like they have since primordial time. The whole idea of inanimate objects picking and choosing how to interact with the physical world is an absurdity, an insane concept. Sasha has a trained mind. She graduated from MIT, first in her class. I don't understand how such nonsense could take root in a scientific mindset like hers. She must be under pressure. Something has to be affecting her thought patterns. I've never known her to be irrational.

Carl pushed through the huge double glass doors at the front entrance to his building and waved hello to the receptionist as he walked past her polished aluminum and chrome desk.

I suppose aluminum and chromium could melt at higher temperatures if they weren't dominated by physical law and solidify days later, according to Sasha.

After entering his office, Carl walked to his computer and powered it up. His routine had been the same every morning for the past seven years. He would check his email messages, look over the snail mail from the previous day, and listen to his voicemail messages immediately after arrival in the office. It was the only way to keep from ignoring them altogether. Carl's dislike for mail was only surpassed by his hatred for telephone messages. His days quickly became intense and so focused on the latest research project that sometimes, gnawing hunger pains were the only clues to eat, and avoiding communication from extraneous sources was the norm. He was cited a year ago for his work on the creation of the metabolic chamber, which allows people to simply step inside and temporarily speed up their metabolism and burn off calories. His latest project includes the development of a chemical substance that breaks down toxic waste and renders it harmless. Carl notices an email message from Sasha. He toys with the idea of ignoring it and getting to work but can't resist the thought of Sasha and her good looks.

"Meet me for lunch. I want to introduce you to someone who has some more detailed info about the idea we discussed last night. Let's say around noon at The Cliché?"

"Okay, but I hope it makes more sense than what you told me last night," he responded.

"It does. Just you wait and see," Sasha replied.

Carl signed off on his email to Sasha and set his cell phone to alarm him at 11:45. He was curious to hear what she had to say, and he didn't want to be late. Promptness was a devotion of his. He had been that way since childhood, and while a grad student at Stanford developed skill at time management and performance, which helped him earn the school's highest academic honors. It was however, a family trait. Everyone in his family was punctual, and the Mathews clan had earned a reputation for reliability in Cincinnati. His dad was the first African American chief of police in the City's history, and his mother was a teacher.

Carl jumped into his research project, ignoring everything else until the alarm on his cell phone buzzed inside his jacket pocket. He quickly shut things down and gave his assistants a little extra time for lunch. The Cliché was about a ten-minute walk from the lab, and he needed the exercise. Physical activity was the one thing he had been neglecting lately, and the little pouch developing around his mid-section was proof positive. Arriving a little early, he decided to get a table before Sasha got there. He couldn't stand the idea of passing up an available table and perhaps having to wait even longer after Sasha arrived. Carl was ushered to a booth near the entrance, which allowed him to look for Sasha and wave her over when she arrived.

He was a little surprised to see her enter, accompanied by a gentleman in a suit and tie. Carl had a little crush on Sasha that had never been acknowledged. Her good looks were obvious, but her mind was the attraction for him. He understood her to be absolutely brilliant, and that had always been the turn-on for him. His heart always skipped a little beat when he set eyes on her, and the corner of his mouth usually turned upward in a little smile. She was one of nine children born to a struggling black family in Washington D.C., all of whom had graduated from college.

Carl stood as she approached the table, greeted her, and stretched out his hand when she introduced him to Professor Hill, a scientist from MIT who had contacted Sasha about work he had been doing. She had completed background research while she was at MIT that triggered his new project. Sasha scooted into the booth next to Carl, and Professor Hill took the seat opposite both of them. A waiter joined them tableside, and after each of them ordered, Professor Hill extracted a handful of papers from his briefcase and spread them on the table so that Carl and Sasha could see them.

"Carl, Sasha tells me that you are not a believer in the Anti Homeostasis Theory."

"That is an understatement, Professor Hill. I don't see how anyone could believe it."

"I have some documentation here that just might change your mind. We know that there are some very strange things going on, and we've investigated them, and have some results that bear witness to how some chemical elements have begun to behave strangely, to disobey the physical laws of the universe."

"What does that mean, Professor Hill? How does a chemical disobey? You're using language that doesn't apply to a non-living thing."

"Actually, Carl, I'm not. When a living or non-living thing is acted upon by the physical laws of the universe, it either succumbs to the action or doesn't. I call that obedience or disobedience. I try not to get hung up on the semantics."

"We live in a part of the universe where everything follows the laws of nature, except for a few chemicals that Professor Hill has discovered," Sasha added.

"And what does that mean?"

"It means that there are some things here from another part of the universe, things that are superior to any earthly object we know," Professor Hill said. "And my research here shows their strange interaction with earthly chemicals."

"Wait a minute. Are you saying that there are alien chemicals on earth, chemicals that no one has categorized?"

"Not only that, Carl, but we have no idea where they come from." Professor Hill said. "The scary thing is that they are dominating every chemical they come in contact with. We are having difficulty containing them. We think there may be more of them here that we don't know about. What it means Carl, is that there are things in parts of the universe that are so far superior to us that we can't even conceptualize them. These chemicals are from the fringe between the dumb part of the universe and the smarter elements. It's like the difference between the first telephone and the latest smartphone."

"And by dumb part of the universe, you mean where everything obeys the laws of nature, like gravity?"

"Yes, but the interesting thing is that we can't get to the higher universe from here, but evidently things from there can come here. And they may have been here for a long time, having their way with the dumb elements, the inferior inhabitants of the lesser part of the universe."

The three of them sat and ate and talked for an hour or so. Sasha and Professor Hill elaborated on their theory as Carl, still unconvinced, listened intently, in between glances at Sasha's pretty brown eyes. As they were concluding their meeting, the waiter returned with a note someone had given him for Professor Hill. Upon reading the note, Professor Hill assured Carl and Sasha he would contact them in a day or so and dashed off to what he described as an urgent meeting.

The abrupt end to lunch with Professor Hill was a little disconcerting to Carl and Sasha. They decided to walk back to work, and on the way out of the restaurant, Carl grabbed a couple of mints from the jar at the entrance and shared with Sasha. On the way back to West Labs, finishing a cool mint, Carl and Sasha found enough interest in each other to change the tenor of their conversation, and Carl asked Sasha out on a date.

"I thought you'd never ask," Sasha said.

"I've wanted to ask you out for a while, but was afraid of offending you. I have a lot of respect for your work and talent and didn't want you to think I couldn't relate to a pretty woman who was also a brilliant scientist without trying to hit on her."

Sasha blushed and smiled.

"Thank you Carl, for the compliment, but I'm glad you overcame your tentativeness. It saved me from jumping your bones in the lab one day."

This time it was Carl's turn to blush and smile, but he didn't stop there. He reached out to Sasha and pulled her close. Her lightly sweet and airy perfume delighted him. Holding her in his arms and looking into her light brown eyes captivated him. He kissed her gently. Both parts of the universe, both smart and dumb, dissolved in the moment. It could have been a minute or two or an hour or two; it could have been a lifetime or two, or three or four. Traffic slowed. Time wobbled.

"Get a room," someone yelled from an open car window.

Everyone in the city could have yelled at them from every vehicle. It would not have mattered. Slowly and dreamily, they pulled back from each other.

"Carl, I could not have imagined you being this passionate."

"It's you, Sasha. Wow, had I only known, I would have done this a long time ago."

"Okay, so you have no excuse now."

"You're right, Sasha. What are you doing for the rest of your life?"

"What-the rest of my life? What are you saying, Carl?"

"Whoa, I don't know? Did I just say that? I think I just asked you to marry me. I must be losing my mind. Speaking of chemistry and elements dominating other elements."

Sasha's heart was beating as fast as a humming bird's wings in flight. She was flushed and warm all over.

"Do we want to stop and think for a moment about this?" she asked.

"Just say yes, and then we can take the time to think about how and when."

"Yes, yes, absolutely yes."

Carl and Sasha embraced again, sealing their commitment. The air swirled softly around them. Everything had changed instantly for them, and the idea of distant parts of the universe couldn't be further from their minds. They strolled, meandered back to West Labs, holding hands, silently. Carl would be late getting back to work from lunch for the first time in his life, and it didn't matter to him. His lab assistants were almost ready to call 911.

Carl and Sasha hugged and kissed again at the receptionist's desk and made plans for dinner that evening to discuss the beginning of their lives together. When Carl arrived back in his office, several people rushed to him asking if he was okay, asking if he had been in a car accident, had he been ill.

"No, I got engaged. I asked Sasha Jones to marry me."

Everyone was taken aback immediately. It was unbelievable for a guy like Carl. They all thought of him as a serious-minded scientist who would be a loner all his life.

"How long have you two been dating?" one of his assistants asked.

Carl looked at his watch. "About an hour and a half," he said.

Their mouths were all agape. Instant love was just not an idea any of them would associate with Carl. He walked over to his desk and plopped down in his chair, contemplating the events that took place over the last two hours and couldn't help wondering how things could have happened so fast.

Dumb part of the universe? Am I from the dumb part of the planet? What just happened?

Buyer's remorse was fleeting. The impression of Sasha's lips on his was indelible. He sat daydreaming for a moment or two before his lab assistants came inquiring about moving on with their work.

"Carry on," Carl said. "I have a new research project that I'm tinkering with. I need some time to ferret out the basics, to conceptualize, as it were."

Thinking that aliens must have abducted Carl and left a substitute in his place, his assistants walked away, puzzled, and yet determined to continue on the project they had begun under his earlier tutelage. In another part of the building, a similar situation had played itself out. Sasha had demurred on continuing work she should have begun upon entering her lab, and sat daydreaming at her desk. Unable to enlist her direction, her lab assistants carried on without her.

"Sasha, what just happened?" Carl asked when she answered her cell phone.

"I don't know. It was like something just took over my senses, and I was swept away. We need to meet right away, so we can see if it happens again."

"I agree. Can you meet me in the stairwell between the fifth and sixth floors in ten minutes?"

"Yes, I'll be there."

Carl and Sasha explained away their needs to leave the labs and headed toward the stairwell. Sasha entered from the sixth floor, and Carl entered from the fifth and approached each other panting. They immediately embraced and kissed.

"Damn, that was great," Carl said. "But it wasn't quite like before." Sasha grabbed his face between her hands, and passionately kissed him again.

"Wow, you're right, Carl. That was amazing, but I didn't feel like I was going to faint as I did earlier. Don't get me wrong, I loved it, but something is different."

"Well, it could be the fact that we're making out in the stairwell like two teenagers, but that should make it all the more exciting," Carl said. "What's different, Sasha?"

"I don't know, but we need to figure it out."

They sat on the steps and began a lengthy discussion about the day's events, exhausting every minute detail. They had no answers except for the fact that the common denominator was Professor Hill. Sasha reached for her cell phone and dialed up Professor Hill, who was anxious to talk to her and Carl. They arranged to meet him right away. Although things seemed different, Carl and Sasha realized that they had been holding hands throughout the conversation on the back stairwell. Whatever happened, the spark was lit, and they could see it in each other's eyes.

The drive to Dr. Hill's office was short and silent. Carl and Sasha were pensive, debating with their rational selves about the reality of the past several hours. Before getting out of the car, they paused and looked into each other's eyes.

"One more time Sasha. Tell me if it's real," Carl said as he pulled her close and kissed her deeply.

"Oh, that was real enough for me," Sasha said, gasping for air.

As they kissed again, a rap on the car window interrupted their amorous embrace.

"Hello in there. Hello," the parking lot attendant said. "That's five dollars, and leave your keys, please."

Embarrassed, Carl and Sasha exited the car and headed for Dr. Hill's office. They walked down a long hallway and up a short pair of steps and through the entrance of a dimly lit and empty outer office to Dr. Hill's back laboratory.

"Ah, my friends, I've been expecting you. Please come in."

"Why? Why were you expecting to see us?" Carl asked.

"In due time young man in due time. First, I must examine your eyes. Please come into the light?"

"Whoa, hold on. What is this about? I'm not submitting to an examination. What going on?" Carl said.

"Oh, I'm afraid you've already submitted, maybe not to an examination, but to a more powerful and intelligent force. That is what pushed the two of you together, uncontrollably."

"Are you saying what I think you're saying? Sasha asked.

"I've always known you to be intuitive, Sasha, but let me put your mind at ease. I've been working with some unstable chemicals and before I left the lab this morning to meet the two of you, I discovered what I believed to be a concoction that has been around for years but only referred to in song and myth. You've no doubt heard of Love Potion Number 9. I have isolated and combined its components. The two of you got a bit of it in your drinks at The Cliché. I paid the waiter to do it for me."

Professor Hill pulled a small glass bottle out of his lab coat and placed it on the counter beside where they were standing.

"It came from this vial here."

"What? You drugged us?" Carl asked angrily. "How dare you. We should bring you up on charges here at the university."

"I must confess and beg your forgiveness, but it is part of a larger puzzle. These chemicals are part of what I described as elements from another part of the universe that dominates lesser molecules here on earth and have done so for millions of years. It is certainly your prerogative to file charges against me, but I was hoping that two extraordinary scientists such as yourselves would understand the importance and significance of my work."

"Of course we understand," Sasha said. But that does not mean we aren't upset with your egregious violations and the liberties you took. You should be ashamed of yourself."

"You are right, my dear, but did you two not fall instantly and madly in love with each other? What of that? Can the sins of Cupid ever be forgiven? Is love not a gift, however it arrives?"

Carl and Sasha were puzzled as to a response to Dr. Hill's questions, yet still enthralled with each other and unsure whether the love potion or an inevitable, irrevocable desire for each other was responsible for their current feelings. Dr. Hill pulled a small green vial out of his pocket and placed it next to the potion on the counter.

"I have an antidote here. Do you want me to administer it, or do you want to remain in love forever? At times there may be an ebb and flow to the power of the chemicals over you, but without the antidote, they will never lose their effect."

"We've fallen in love, but a great deal of it was us, not some damn love potion, wasn't it, Carl?"

Carl dared not say no, because of his feelings for Sasha, but his scientific, rational mind told him that a factual chemical answer was more reliable than his passion for her.

"Carl. What do you think?" she asked again, this time with her hands on her hips as she tapped the floor with her shoe.

Before Carl could answer, an elderly and portly cleaning woman pushing a cart full of supplies entered Dr. Hill's lab. She excused herself for interrupting their conversation and asked Dr. Hill if he wanted her to clean the floor in his office. He told her no, but there was something he wanted to show her to clean in his office. They stepped away for a moment. Carl noticed that Dr. Hill had a cup of what appeared to be coffee on the counter. It was still hot to the touch. He looked at the two vials of chemicals on the counter with a raised eyebrow. Sasha saw a gleam in his eye as he reached for the vial containing the potion.

"No, you wouldn't."

"Why not?" Carl replied as he opened the potion and added a drop to Dr. Hill's coffee cup.

Professor Hill returned and immediately took a sip from his cup.

"Look, Dr. Hill. We have not made up our minds yet. Let us take the antidote with us, and if we decide to use it we will do so over the weekend and bring it back on Monday."

"Fine, Carl. I guess that's reasonable. Please give me a call Monday morning." Carl took the antidote and placed it in his pocket as he and Sasha said goodbye. Dr. Hill continued sipping at his coffee as the cleaning lady called him.

"Dr. Hill, can you come here please?"

"Of course, of course," he said, drinking more coffee.

Sasha and Carl paused at the door to the lab. Momentarily they heard giggles and an exclamation coming from Dr. Hill's office.

"Oh, Professor. Oh my."

One Declines

Curtis, an exceptionally hip but graying male Praying Mantis, and Barry, a

recently mature Mantis, lounge upon a small rock in a vacant lot near the edge of

the city.

"Hey man, those two cuties over there are winking at us. Let's hop over and

get acquainted," Barry says.

"Whoa young boy," Curtis cautions. "I haven't lived to this ripe old age by chasing Praying Mantis chicks. You need to slow down and consider your options. I prefer grasshoppers myself."

"I heard that about you, man. Are you nuts?"

"No, and if you want to keep yours, you'd better reconsider your plans."

"I guess what they say about you is true," Barry says. "My mother warned me about you. She said you were no good for Mantisville, and that Mantises like you could be the end of us all."

"Okay, Barry, let me ask you this? What does your father say about me?"

"My father ain't around. He took off like all the other male Mantises in the community."

"Took off, as in had his head taken off when your mother chowed down on his ass before you were hatched."

"Take that back old man, or I'll kick your ass," Barry says, flaring his nostrils.

"Hey, don't hate the messenger. I'm only spreading the truth homeboy. Has no one told you about this whole mating ritual thing? The female Mantis will literally bite your head off when the mating ritual is over and then devour the rest of your body."

"I've heard rumors, but they're all bullshit."

"How do you know? Look around you. Answer these two questions. How come the only male Praying Mantises, except me, that are still alive around here are youngsters? Why am I the only old guy still alive around here? If you answer them correctly, you'll change your mind about that little cute Praying Mantis trying to get your attention over there."

Barry Mantis pauses for a moment or two but is unable to resist the attraction to the female beckoning him to join her. As he begins to hop over to her side, Curtis tries one more time to dissuade him.

"Don't do it, man. Listen, I have a date with a green stick leaf insect tonight who has a really fine ass cousin. I can make sure she's invited along so you can meet her."

"No thanks, man. I see what I want," Barry responds, jumping over twigs and vegetation.

"Okay. I'll remember you to your offspring."

Curtis coolly strolls back to his pad to prepare for his date, glancing over the teeming insect life in the vacant lot.

Sometimes being a bug in the city ain't pretty, but at least I can go to dinner tonight without becoming part of the menu.

Tongue in Cheek

To say that Odell Harper was a mean son-of-a-gun would be like saying toxic nuclear waste may be harmful if swallowed. He was equally feared and hated in the community he loosely called home and often walked with both fists balled up. Only his mother loved him, but then only until he was about four years old. Mumbling under her breath that she couldn't take it anymore, she set fire to his birth certificate when he was eleven years old and abandoned him in the parking lot of the all-night Dollar Store. Immediately after she left, he broke into three parked cars and stole everything of value. A day or so later, he took up residence in the abandoned trailer of an eighteen-wheeler parked in a vacant lot that was surrounded by enough overgrown weeds and junk to make it difficult to see. Harper was big enough and intimidating enough at an early age to make all but the roughest thugs in the hood cross the street rather than pass him on the sidewalk. He was a teenage threat, a menace, and a thorn in the side of a distressed black community, reeling from years of maligned neglect by city, state and federal governments, and a business community that had never had its best interests at heart.

Harper acted alone much of the time until it occurred to him that an accomplice would expand on his ability to take what he wanted from those unable to defend themselves. He found a willing cohort in a young punk named Calvin Peeks. Thin, unwashed, and disheveled most of the time, Peeks was also cowardly and sneaky and took comfort in how folks treated him when he was with Odell Harper. Peeks was also considered the village idiot, and much of the time fell prey to his own poorly hatched schemes and scams. Harper and Peeks became known as Take and Sneak in the community, and gradually became familiar with the feel of handcuffs and the back of police squad cars. They both developed extensive rap sheets and spent considerable time at juvenile detention centers in their developmental years.

One such encounter at a detention center contributed to and extended the feared reputation of Odell. He had been convicted of multiple counts of assault and battery and had been sentenced to serve a year at Burton Detention Center, the last stop before prison for juvenile offenders. It contained a collection of the worst of the worst kind of juvenile delinquents, those considered hardcore and most likely to end up doing hard time in the penitentiary. Odell, about six feet three inches tall at the time and weighing a whopping two hundred and fifty-five pounds, had just been processed into the joint shortly before his seventeenth birthday. He was in line with inmates headed for the lunchroom when he was approached by a guy everyone called Jawbones Jones, who got his name by hurting scores of people with the overly large knuckles on both of his hands.

Jawbones was doing a bit for aggregated assault and burglary. He was a constant

figure in the center's population, and all of the inmates were afraid of him.

"Hey, big boy, I want your lunch," Jawbones said, "When you git your tray,

bring it over and put it on my table."

"You got jokes, hunh? You some kinda comedian?"

"You got to learn to do what I say do," Jones said as he stepped in front of

Odell. He grabbed Odell's arm. "You gotta git more muscle than this to take me

on fat boy."

Jawbones had oversized hands but he hadn't taken the time to notice that

Harper's were much bigger than his. They were huge, thick and heavy, big

enough to hold a basketball in one hand like it was a Cantaloupe. Odell observed

that they were standing next to a metal post in the hallway that housed a loud-

speaker mounted on its top. Odell pulled loose from Jawbones' grip, reached out

and grabbed his arm with his left hand, and pressed the elbow against the post. He

pushed hard against Jones's upper body with his other hand, and everyone within

earshot heard the snap as Jawbones' arm broke. Odell quickly grabbed Jones's

other arm, spun him around, and snapped it against the post. Jawbones collapsed

on the ground, but Odell wasn't finished. He stomped on Jones' left rib cage,

collapsing it beneath the weight of his heavy young body.

"Anybody else want my lunch?" Odell yelled. Not only did he have no takers,

but everyone in line filed past Jones in a heap on the floor as if they had seen and

heard nothing. Jawbones was soon taken to the hospital ward and never returned to prominence in the center. Taking out the top dog in the joint made Odell the new overdog, and he quickly seized on every opportunity to enjoy his new status. That incident created the backdrop for several years of violent fights and the building of a reputation for viciousness unprecedented in the entire city. When he was sent to prison for grand larceny, he encountered a number of older prisoners who challenged him simply because of his history, and it wasn't long before he was running the inmate population. There was one final attempt to bring Harper down that made him a legend among legends in the penitentiary.

He was coming out of the laundry where he had been working for a month or so. It was the end of the shift, and inmates usually left together in groups of around a dozen, but Odell was the only one exiting through the laundry's large double doors. He immediately suspected that something was wrong and stopped to look around. Fifteen feet directly ahead of him were four of the biggest, toughest, and rotten to the core prisoners in the joint approaching him on a collision path. He stepped back into the laundry and yanked the metal handle out of a floor mop, and as the four inmates charged through the doors, proceeded to beat them severely about the head and shoulders, substituting his monster fists now and again for the metal handle. Soon they were in a pile at his feet. He picked each of them up, stuffed them into the dryers, and turned them on. Not wanting to get more time for the murder of four inmates, Harper informed the first guard he saw that there were four prisoners taking a ride inside a couple of the laundry's dryers.

From that day forward, Odell Harper was convinced that brute force, fear, and intimidation were his only marketable assets and the only things between him and his demise. Upon his release from prison, he became a walking, talking crime wave. He learned enough in prison to enable him to skirt capture by law enforcement, and the spoils from his misadventures were enough to allow him to afford an apartment and a workable means of transportation. The building in which he lived quickly became offlimits to most community residents: a location to avoid at all costs. Unfortunately, there were some who couldn't avoid it, like mail carriers and those whose financial condition dictated there was no other option available but to live there in fear of Odell Harper, and the thugs who hung around the building like insects stuck on flypaper.

Wanda Mallard had been employed by the postal service for several years and became the carrier recently assigned the route, which included Odell's residence. She was young, attractive, and hard-working, usually finishing her delivery route early, except for the first day she had to deliver mail to Harper.

It was a Wednesday. Smoke grey clouds drifted slowly over the city. People and things moved at a slow mid-week pace, except for Wanda Mallard. She was moving quickly and was almost done with her deliveries. One more stop, and she would be on her way home to prepare a special meal for her son. It was his birthday.

"Hey sugar, you got somethin' for me?" Odell asked, standing in the doorway of his apartment building.

"If I do, I'll put it in your box," Wanda replied. "If you let me do my job."

"I got somethin I want to put in your box, baby."

Wanda tried to ignore Odell and walked by him over to the building's mailboxes. He watched her walk past, but reached out with his left hand and pulled her close to him. He put his right hand over her mouth, and it nearly covered her whole face. He picked her up as she kicked and flailed her arms, trying to get away from him. His enormous hand covered her mouth and nose, and she was having difficulty breathing. His apartment was immediately behind where he had been standing, and he backed into its open door and kicked it shut. He turned and slammed her against the wall so hard it knocked her unconscious, and she fell to the floor.

Wanda lay sprawled out on the rug atop weeks of paper and trash. Odell stood back as if to admire his prey, a tiny, helpless, unconscious human thing that was now his to use and abuse as he pleased.

Later, much later, disoriented, hurt, clothes torn, Wanda wobbled into the street several blocks away from Odell Harper's apartment and fell to her knees. Cars screeched to a halt, narrowly avoiding her.

"He, he raped me, he raped me," she yelled.

A young woman and an elderly gentleman rushed to her aid in the middle of the street. "I'm calling 911 right now," the woman said as two other passersby helped her to the sidewalk. Moments later, sirens wailed into the intersection at

Fifth and Knoll streets. Wanda was helped into an ambulance and rushed to the hospital.

"He raped me. He raped me," Wanda said over and over again, as she was being administered to in the hospital. "I, I couldn't breathe, his hands, they smothered my face." The police arrived and took her statement. They knew all too well whom she was talking about and immediately afterward arrested Odell Harper for suspicion of rape and aggravated assault and battery.

The weeks and months that followed the incident did not go well for Wanda Mallard. She had been so traumatized by her ordeal that she became despondent and almost non-communicative. She didn't return to work and soon left the city to recuperate in Georgia with her sister. The case against Odell Harper fell apart without her participation and testimony, and he was never brought to trial for his misdeeds. Community residents were convinced of his guilt and wanted nothing more than to see him punished for his crimes against her and them. There was talk of forming a vigilante group and taking the law into their own hands, but it was only talk. No one wanted to tangle with him, and his cohorts and no one wanted to risk spending time in jail for meting out justice to such low-life individuals.

Odell Harper was free to carry on with his larcenous ways, until he collapsed on the sidewalk in front of the drug store one afternoon after a morning spent intimidating and harassing teenagers walking to the local high school. Community residents who passed him lying in a heap on the concrete cheered and clapped as though he had just given an award-winning performance. Many of them whipped out their cell phones, snapped pictures with the cameras, and posted them on every social media site available. He would have remained there for days had it not been for the fact that his huge body was partially blocking entrance to the drug store. The store owner called 911, and the police and an ambulance arrived to take Odell to the hospital.

In the emergency room, he was diagnosed with acute appendicitis. They surmised that his appendix had burst and he needed surgery immediately to save his life. They rushed him to operating room A113 as the hospital paging system announced, "Dr. Gideon, Dr. Walter Gideon to operating room A113, Dr. Gideon to operating room A113."

Walter Gideon, a talented and skilled surgeon,was on duty at the county hospital. He was known for innovation and precision. He arrived in the operating room just as they were wheeling Odell Harper through the doors. Dr. Gideon froze in mid-stride. "Is this who needs my help, this guy?" he asked.

"Yes, doctor," the nurse said as she read the paperwork in her hand. "Odell, Harper."

Gideon was incredulous at the prospect of performing this procedure, particularly since he was Wanda Mallard's older brother and recognized Harper as the man he knew had raped his little sister. His conscience, and the Hippocratic Oath he had taken when he became a physician suddenly slammed into the revenge he had sworn he would exact on the monster responsible for the horrendous crimes against his baby sister. His thoughts were all over the place.

"What the? This can't be true. Oh, my God. It's him, the beast, and he's at my mercy. What do I do, leave an instrument in his body, accidentally snip an artery? Should I just allow him to die on the operating table? Do I repair this bastard's body and let him resume his reign of terror in the city? My little sister, what this creep did to her. I can't let him get away with it anymore."

Hours later, they rolled Odell Harper out of the operating room and into the recovery ward. The attending nurse noticed that his neck had been bandaged and thought it a little strange since the operation was to remove the patient's appendix, but she didn't question the procedure; besides, Harper had tubes up his nose, down his throat and an IV in his arm. Anything could have happened while the patient went under the knife.

Walter Gideon left instructions to keep Harper sedated a little more than what was necessary. It would be a few days before Odell would consciously relate to the world again. He had no reason to anyway. No one would come to visit him, and no one would miss him in the outside world. His only friend, Calvin Peeks, was finishing a short stint in the workhouse and would not be released for a while. So, Odell Harper laid recuperating and resting in the county hospital recovery ward, unaware of the reality he would soon awake to.

It was 8 AM on a Tuesday morning and nurse Lela Carson stood over Odell Harper checking his vital signs. His eyes opened, and he tried to sit up.

"Careful now, you've been through a lot. Take it easy. You're in pretty good shape. I'm sure the doctor will release you in a day or so, and you can go home. Is there anything I can get you now?" the nurse asked, but the response from Odell Harper was certainly not what she had expected.

"Mmmph capph ungggg," were the muffled sounds he made as his lips moved, but the sounds came from somewhere else.

"What? I can't understand what you said."

Again Lela Carson heard muffled sounds as Harper's lips moved.

"Ssskkss, fusshh, nooosshh."

"Wait, are you a ventriloquist? I can see your lips moving, but the sound is coming from underneath you. Be still. Something's wrong. I need to turn you over, but you'll have to help me. Gently now, turn on your side."

Odell turned on his side, and Nurse Carson noticed a small dressing covering a small portion of his buttocks, right in the middle of both cheeks.

"What is this? I didn't see any indication of a procedure back here on your charts. I'm going to remove this dressing. Please be still."

When she removed the gauze, she was still puzzled. "I'm confused. What happened back here?" she said and almost fainted when Odell spoke, and the sound wafted from his rear end, from exactly between both cheeks.

"What's wrong? What's goin on?" Odell asked as he tried to get up but was still not strong enough to stand and fell back onto the bed.

Nurse Carson dropped the dressing and ran out of the ward. Moments later, she ran back into the ward with two resident physicians in tow and rushed over to Harper's bed. They pulled the curtain around his bed and asked him to turn over so they could examine his backside. Odell was in a strange predicament. He wanted to perform his ape shit routine and fly into a rage and pummel anyone and everyone within striking distance of his enormous fists but was too weak, and for the first time since he could remember was unable to be intimidating.

"Okay, can you speak for us?" one of the doctors asked.

Again Odell tried to speak from his mouth, but the words marched from between his pursed butt cheeks as the doctors, and Lela Carson watched and listened. They were astonished, and even though they saw and heard what happened were not ready to accept what had transpired until they asked Odell to speak again.

"That's amazing. I still can't believe it. I didn't know it was even possible to do something like that. This is a medical phenomenon. You're going to be famous, Mr. Harper," one of the doctors said.

"Famous my ass. You have to fix this," Odell said from between his butt cheeks.

The examinations and inquiries that followed established the facts. Dr. Walter Gideon had removed Odell Harper's vocal cords from his throat and not only placed them at the opening of his rectum but made them function when he moved his lips. It was an ingenious and brilliant surgical procedure, a marvel of technical skill and precision, but one that brought Gideon praise and condemnation. He could not be found, however, not in the continental United States. He had escaped to an island paradise somewhere in the South Pacific. His sister, Wanda Mallard, was buoyed by the news he had relayed to her before he left the country. It would go far in helping her to recuperate and regain her emotional health. Odell Harper was told that there could be no attempt to reverse the procedure that had been performed on him until Walter Gideon was found. What had been done was so technically beyond the skills and knowledge of any other living surgeon. Soon Harper was released from the hospital and tried in every way possible to hide the results of Gideon's procedure.

Late Saturday afternoon, the week after his release from the hospital, as the sun was slowly losing its grip on a wall of blue sky and clouds, Odell Harper casually strolled down Seventh Street toward his crib when his cell phone rang. He retrieved it from his pocket but realized that speaking on it would be a problem with the number of other people who were in close proximity to him. He saw what he thought was an opportunity to talk on his phone and not be seen. He ducked down the alley between Seventh and Eighth Streets, looked around and seeing no one, placed his phone on the back of his pants, and said, "Hey, talk to me." In order to hear what the caller was saying, he removed the phone from the back of his pants and placed it on his ear. He repeated this behavior, alternating the phone from his ear to his ass, over and over during the cell phone conversation he was having. After completing his call, he looked around, up and down the alley, then sauntered back onto Seventh Street.

Unbeknownst to him, a young girl who had been sitting on her window sill on the second floor of the building directly across from where he had been standing, not only observed what she thought was weirdly comical behavior, but recorded it on her cell phone's video camera. She thought it was so funny that she shared it over the Internet with one of her girlfriends who urged her to upload it to You-Tube, which she did post-haste.

Soon the whole world had access to Odell's alley exhibition as the video went viral in a matter of a few days. Odell did not interface with any kind of social media and remained oblivious to the YouTube video. Word traveled fast, however, in the community, and although no one would make fun of Odell Harper to his face, many laughed at him, behind his back. No one dared challenge him but gradually, accidents began to happen to him. Objects fell out of second and third-floor windows on his head as he walked past apartment buildings. Cars swerved narrowly missing him as he crossed the street, and one day, he became the target of a drive-by shooting, which made him fly into a rage.

He jumped aboard a city bus that pulled up to the corner and grabbed the first person in sight and pinned him against the bus window. Odell was so angry that he forgot about his physical condition and yelled at the frightened little man in his grasp.

"Why's everybody tryin' to kill me? You know. Tell me or I'll snap your neck."

His lips moved but the loud, angry words flew out of the space between the back pockets of his jeans. The person directly across the aisle asked if Odell was talking to him.

"Do I look like I'm talkin' to you?" Odell asked as he turned to face the other passenger, but his words were aimed elsewhere.

"I, I can't tell. Your lips are movin', but the sound is comin' from somewhere else."

Realizing that he had revealed his bizarre communication problem to a whole busload of passengers, Odell stopped his aggressive behavior and got off of the bus, but the truth had been told. He walked angrily home, hoping someone would get in his way so that he could take out his vengeance on him or her. Shortly after arriving home, Calvin Peeks knocked on his door. He had just been released from prison. Once inside, he turned his cell phone on and brought YouTube up on the screen.

"Hey, man you gotta see this," he said. "I heard about it in the joint. All the cats on my cellblock were talkin' about it. It's a video on YouTube and it shows you doin' some strange stuff in the alley with your cell phone. You seen it yet?"

Odell snatched the phone out of Peeks' hand, watched the video in disbelief, and became so angry that he threw his only friend in the world out of his place. In the days and weeks that followed, Odell Harper became increasingly reclusive. It was almost as if he were hiding, ashamed to show his face. His demeanor began to change dramatically. The once defiant Odell Harper, the man for whom adversity and gangs, and guns, and violence were no match was succumbing to something he could neither hit with his fists nor scare away. It was ghostly and beyond his ability to dispatch. The brute that feared nothing and no one was becoming vulnerable. Something was eating away at his psyche. The humiliation he felt on the bus, and the shame that totally absorbed him when he viewed the YouTube video of himself talking on his cell phone in the alley between Eighth and Seventh Streets was psychologically disabling.

The angry, intimidating, fearless bully, the abuser, the rapist, shrank behind the walls of his tiny apartment until he climbed out of his window one night and wandered off, slinking sideways down alleys and dark streets. He hid under bridges and in abandoned homes in city after city. One day, as he held a sign and begged for money on a highway exit ramp, a circus performer recognized him and convinced him to join his company's sideshow. Soon, he was part of the Iron Ring Traveling Circus, and performed for dimes and quarters, as "The World's Only Real Live Talking Asshole."

The Ode-ification of Buster Willis

A little bit of sun

A little bit of moon

A little bit of time

Left in June

And no one saw Buster stumble into the alleyway

fall beneath the wired branches of planted telephone poles rowed behind useless garages overflowing garbage cans dried river beds of comingled blood urine framing an old tennis shoe laying on its side it seemed bizarre that its worn out sole and Buster's would come to rest in the same wasteland of forgotten things of displaced discarded things

A little bit of sun

A little bit of moon

A little bit of time

Left in June

And Buster Willis gone way too soon

Unforgettable

The pungency of the city

flares your nostrils

seeps inside

dances on your bones

makes you taste it at the cellular level

strokes your genes

settles

in tomorrow's dreams

We Struggle We Live

We are from here

the city of

broken homes

broken sidewalks

broken dreams

broken promises

broken hearts

and are a people yet unbroken

Made in the USA
Monee, IL
03 February 2020